"Not danc... Gavin asked, smiling.

Some imp of mischief inspired her to be flirtatious. "Oh, I've been waiting for you."

"I'll pretend to believe that," he said, taking her hand.

Judith wasn't used to such assertive men, but rather than make a scene, she allowed herself to be led onto the dance floor. Her hackles were up, though, and he seemed to sense that as he drew her into his arms.

"I'm not usually so peremptory," he said.

"Oh? *I'll* pretend to believe *that*."

They looked at each other challengingly for a moment, then abruptly relaxed and laughed. "Something tells me we're well matched," he said, without a hint of chagrin.

Dear Reader,

When two people fall in love, the world is suddenly new and exciting, and it's that same excitement we bring to you in Silhouette Intimate Moments. These are stories with scope, with grandeur. These characters lead the lives we all dream of, and everything they do reflects the wonder of being in love.

Longer and more sensuous than most romances, Silhouette Intimate Moments novels take you away from everyday life and let you share the magic of love. Adventure, glamour, drama, even suspense— these are the passwords that let you into a world where love has a power beyond the ordinary, where the best authors in the field today create stories of love and commitment that will stay with you always.

In coming months look for novels by your favorite authors: Maura Seger, Parris Afton Bonds, Elizabeth Lowell and Erin St. Claire, to name just a few. And whenever you buy books, look for all the Silhouette Intimate Moments, love stories *for* today's women *by* today's women.

Leslie J. Wainger
Senior Editor
Silhouette Books

IMRL-7/85

Maura Seger

Happily Ever After

Silhouette Intimate Moments

Published by Silhouette Books New York

America's Publisher of Contemporary Romance

SILHOUETTE BOOKS
300 East 42nd St., New York, N.Y. 10017

ISBN: 0-373-07176-0

First Silhouette Books printing January 1987

MAURA SEGER

was prompted by a love of books and a vivid imagination to decide, at age twelve, to be a writer. Twenty years later, her first book was published. So much, she says, for overnight success! Now each book is an adventure, filled with fascinating people who always surprise her.

Chapter 1

The New York Times

Cambridge, Massachusetts. Scientists at the Massachusetts Institute of Technology today announced the discovery of a new isotope called xanium, which has the ability to focus high-energy beams on distant, moving targets. The discovery could significantly affect the development of an anti-nuclear "umbrella" in space. However, a spokesman for the team that made the discovery warned that xanium is extremely rare and that efforts to create it artificially in the laboratory have proved to be completely unsuccessful.

Cosmopolitan Magazine

Royal Romance in Fairy-Tale Gregoria! Feminine hearts are breaking as news comes that His Royal Highness King Gregory XXIII will soon be a bachelor no more. His Highness, renowned as a championship racing car driver and polo player, will wed the lovely Lady Althea Desiree. The ceremony, next month in the capital city of the enchanting medieval kingdom, promises to be *the* social event of the decade. Move over, Charles and Di, there's soon to be a new royal couple on the scene!

The Washington Post

The White House announced today the nomination of Gavin Penderast, currently assistant Secretary of State for Middle Eastern Affairs, as United States Ambassador to the Kingdom of Gregoria. Mr. Penderast is a career diplomat, a former Marine Corps pilot, and a recipient of the Medal of Honor. His appointment is expected to receive congressional approval without delay.

Variety

Scuttlebutt in TV land is that news correspondent Judith Fairchild is headed home to Gotham from L.A. for a *big* job at the network level. With UBC's top anchorman hinting at retirement, execs have their eyes out

for a boffo replacement. Judith just might be
it. Since she broke the story on last year's
Libyan plutonium theft, the leggy blond
beauty has been taken *very* seriously indeed.

"And I damn well intend to keep on being taken seriously," Judith said as she tossed the copy of *Variety*
onto her boss's desk and glared at him. "I didn't come
all the way back to New York, and a job at the network, in order to report on some Ruritanian wedding!"

"Take it easy," Sam Wexman said. He was a mid-
dle-aged man of medium height with thinning brown
hair, soulful eyes, and a resilient paunch that resisted
all efforts at dieting and exercise. He dressed nonde-
scriptly, listened more than he talked, and had few
enemies in an industry where the rule was if you
couldn't say something nasty about someone, you
didn't say anything.

On first meeting him, people tended to underesti-
mate Sam. They overlooked the fact that he had
crawled his way to the pinnacle of network news power
in a twenty-year career that had been through two
wars, social upheaval, and the demise of more than a
few men who had presumed themselves to be far more
talented than the quiet Sam Wexman. They were gone;
he remained. Judith was too smart not to know what
that meant, but it didn't stop her from being one very
angry lady.

"This isn't why I came here, Sam," she said, turning around to stare out the floor-to-ceiling window.

This afforded Sam a view of her long, slender body clad in an ivory silk shirt, brown lizard skin belt, narrow taupe skirt, beige stockings, and pumps that matched the belt. Her blond hair—a shade somewhere between honey and caramel—shone in the sunlight. Sam would have been less than a man if he hadn't appreciated the view, but he was careful to keep any sign of that well hidden.

"Tell me why you did come." He leaned back in his oversized leather chair. His feet were propped up on the marble slab that served as his desk. It had been his predecessor's choice, and he hadn't gotten around to replacing it yet. In the two years he'd had the job, he'd been too busy to think of such trivialities. Besides, he'd seen on one of the budget reports that the office furnishings had cost a hundred thousand dollars, and that had so scandalized him that he refused to even paint the place.

"Why I came?" Judith said. She had dragged her attention away from the spectacular Manhattan skyline without much difficulty, since she hadn't really been seeing it anyway. It was getting dark and the lights were coming on in all the buildings, a veritable galaxy of twinkling stars. All over the city, people were pausing to sniff the early spring air and let the essence of New York romance seep into their souls. But not Judith. She had a bone between her teeth and wasn't about to let it go.

"Do we really have to go over this again?" When he didn't respond, she said, "I came here because you offered me regular spots on the network evening news with a range of stories that would whet the appetite of any reporter worthy of the name. Not once, in all those lunches we had in L.A., did you so much as hint that you saw me as some glorified women's features type, some air head to simper about the latest fashions and the two dozen things you can do with marshmallows and hotdogs. Not once, Sam Wexman, did you reveal your true colors. But now that you have I've got a damn good mind to quit!''

Her blue eyes—which one besotted gentleman had likened to the color of the Aegean at sunrise—spat fire at him. Sam took a firmer grip on his armrests and managed a smile. ''Go ahead. But if you do, you'll be running the risk of missing one hell of a story.''

''*That wedding?* Come off it, Sam. It's the Charles and Di show all over again. Even if I did have a thing for white lace and lovebirds, I wouldn't want it in reruns.''

''There's a little bit more involved here.'' He swung his legs off the desk and straightened up. Judith's slanted eyebrows drew together. She had already learned that whenever Sam stopped being deliberately casual, he had something very serious on his mind.

The manila folder that he pushed across the desk toward her was thin and unlabeled. She stared at it as he said, ''Gavin Penderast is going to Gregoria.''

''Bully for him.''

''You don't know who he is?''

"Assistant Secretary for Middle Eastern Affairs. Helped work out the Treaty of Jerusalem. Big name at State, but very secretive."

"Got it on one. The top boys think the world of him. Word is he could be Secretary of State in the not-too-distant future."

Judith frowned. She slumped into the chair across from Sam—or, at least, a woman without such innate grace would have slumped; Judith, more correctly, reclined. "If he's such hot stuff, why is he being shunted over to a backwater like Gregoria?"

Sam gave her a gentle smile. "Exactly what I've been wondering."

"Maybe he stepped out of line. Had one too many martinis at some diplomatic do or romanced the wrong man's wife."

"Don't think so. Penderast is as straight as they come. He's a widower with two small children who manages a hectic work schedule well enough to tuck them into bed every night. If he's got any love life at all, he's very discreet about it. In fact, you might say discreet is his middle name. He's been trusted with some very high-level missions in the past, real delicate stuff that needed special handling. Good old Gavin's come through every time. My guess is he's being asked to do so again."

Judith shook her head slowly. "I know President Harrison goes in for traditional values, but I didn't think that meant all the way back to feudalism. And for anything short of that, you don't go to Gregoria. About the only thing I know about the place is that it's some sort of Brigadoon, frozen in time. No,'' she said decisively, ''Penderast must have screwed up somewhere along the way.''

''Maybe,'' Sam acknowledged, ''and maybe not. Not too many people know this, but our newest ambassador has a master's degree in physics from Cal Tech. Word is he's kept up his interest in it and has some heavy-duty friends working in the field. Including that bunch at M.I.T.''

Judith's eyes widened, giving her for just a moment the look of innocent delight she had had as a child. That was replaced quickly with a shrewd appraisal that had cut through more than one hapless interviewee's best efforts at evasion. ''That's what I like about you, Sam. You get right to the point.''

''So I enjoyed seeing you squirm a little. Now will you go to Gregoria?''

''Maybe. I have to look into it a bit more.'' She stood and reached for the folder. ''I'll let you know in a couple of days.''

''You realize,'' he said, ''that there are people being paid five hundred g's a year who show their bosses a little respect?''

''Wrong,'' she said with a smile as she headed for the door. ''For that insane amount of money you get nothing but unvarnished honesty. If I think there's a story, I'll say so. Same if I don't.''

''Hmmph.'' Her hand was on the knob when Sam added, ''There's a picture of Penderast in that file.''

''So?''

He shrugged. "I just thought you might find it interesting."

"It's the man's mission I'm curious about, nothing else."

"If you say so." He gave her a funny little smile that she forgot about the moment she was out of his office, until she opened the file and saw the photo.

Gavin Penderast was a hunk. A stud, a dish, a dreamboat. However far back you wanted to go in the lexicon of synonyms for gorgeous male, he met the grade. Handsome didn't describe him at all, he went so far beyond it. Judith knew more than her share of attractive men and was not easily impressed. But she spent the first five minutes back at her desk simply staring at the photograph, trying to imagine what the man she saw there might be like.

He was very strong; she saw that at a glance. From the top of his thick ebony hair to his square jaw, sinewy neck, and broad shoulders he personified the virile, self-directed male. His forehead was broad, his eyebrows straight, and his nose assertive. His mouth was surprisingly sensual for so chiseled-looking a man, but that only added to his appeal. Judith allowed herself a purely feminine interlude of appreciation before she turned the photo over and surveyed the first of the neatly typed pages beneath it.

An hour later, she felt that she knew a fair amount about Gavin Penderast, but she wanted to know a great deal more. He was a certified hero, having led the crew of his downed plane to safety across a hundred miles of enemy territory in Vietnam. For that he had received the nation's highest testament to courage, the Congressional Medal of Honor.

The valor he possessed in such abundance must have been severely tested five years before, when his beautiful young wife had been killed in a terrorist attack at the Vienna airport. Judith frowned as she read the description of the tragedy; with her memory jogged, she remembered it quite clearly. Penderast, his wife, and their two children—including a three-month-old baby—had been returning to the States to visit her parents when the assailants struck. In the aftermath, Gavin had resigned his post as Economic Attache at the embassy in Cairo and stayed on in Washington at the State Department. He had risen steadily through the ranks while also caring for his motherless children.

As Sam had said, not a breath of scandal had ever been attached to his name. Indeed, he was widely known as a man of rare perception and fairness. Nonetheless, she was surprised to discover hints that his role in the recent Middle Eastern negotiations, which had concluded with the Treaty of Jerusalem, might well have been even greater than was generally known.

None of which explained what he would be doing in Gregoria.

Judith raised her head and stared out the window, noting absently that it was now dark. The news room was never completely empty, but through her open office door she could see that most of the staff had gone home. Chances were at least a few had popped their heads in to say good-night. She hoped they wouldn't think her rude for not having responded.

She had been completely caught up in Gavin Penderast's story, and suspected that she would remain so for quite some time. Certainly she knew the symptoms well enough. A few times in her professional life—perhaps half a dozen—she had known without being able to say how that she had stumbled across a major story. The Libyan plutonium theft had been one such break, but there had also been others, stretching back to the time when she was a cub reporter on a local station in Talahassee and solved the cases of three missing girls by following a hunch that had led her to their murderer.

That had been almost ten years ago, but she hadn't forgotten the lesson she'd learned, namely to trust her instincts and go with the flow. Sam, darn him, was right. The key was Gregoria, and the easiest way to get there without tipping her hand was to cover the royal wedding. But that didn't mean she had to sink into a veritable treacle of sickening sweetness.

There were ways and then there were ways of covering weddings. She might actually have some fun pulling the wraps off what would undoubtedly be a carefully constructed public facade. After all, these were real people getting hitched, for all that they seemed intent on coming across as characters out of a second-rate operetta. And where there were real people, there was always bound to be trouble.

Cheered by that prospect, she packed up her briefcase, switched off the light and headed for home.

What met that description—temporarily, she hoped—was a two-room apartment on the East Side that was costing her more than her annual salary on her first big job. The walls were paper-thin, the plumbing rattled, and there was only one closet. But, as the effervescent real estate agent had said, "My dear, it has a *river* view."

Two garbage scows were churning their way along the sluggish waterway separating Manhattan from Queens. The latter, like all the boroughs appended onto Manhattan to make up New York, was disdained by every true resident of the glittery island so aptly called Oz on the Hudson. But if Queens cared about that, it didn't show. Lights twinkled on the other side of the river. Ribbons of cars trudged along carrying weary commuters home to their dinners. Judith thought about hers and sighed.

She hated to cook. But then she hated doing most domestic chores. Which, she felt, went at least part of the way toward explaining how she had reached the ripe old age of thirty without ever marrying. Men, no matter how enlightened a line they gave, ultimately expected a woman to look after them. They wanted dinner on the table when they came home, their slippers by the fire, and the children bathed and fed, ready to toddle off to sleep.

Which was a picture she did not care to dwell on, for reasons too painful to contemplate.

She had plans, big ones. Never mind that she had already accomplished far more than most people ever would. She wanted to go a great deal further. Those who speculated that she had her eye on the network anchor chair were right; she intended to be the first woman solo anchor of a nightly network news program, and she intended to do it soon.

Silver-haired, crusty-voiced William Mathers, the network's anchor for the last decade and routinely voted the most trusted man in America, had told her privately that he planned to retire in six months and that he would support her for the job. That was high praise, but then she and Bill had known each other for a long time and had been through some tough spots together. He knew she had what it took, and she knew it, too.

Gregoria could be yet one more stepping stone in ensuring that everyone else got the same message.

What did one wear to a royal wedding? After she had peeled the foil off her dinner and stuck it in the oven, she went into her bedroom and took a look in the closet. Being on camera almost every day required her to have an extensive wardrobe, some of which had been hung in an armoire specially bought for that purpose. Most of the outfits were crisply tailored business suits in colors that flattered her blond hair and light complexion. But there was also a scattering of dresses she wore on those rare occasions when she felt frivolous, and half a dozen evening gowns that got out once or twice a year.

Folded on shelves in the closet was what she thought of as her weekend wardrobe: comfortable old jeans and khakis, soft shirts, and so on. More than once those clothes had been pressed into professional service as she pursued a story over rough ground. Some of her fondest memories involved following leads into the seamier side of whatever town she happened to be in. She had spent her share of time in dives and dumps waiting for an informant to show up, and in the process she had learned more than a little about taking care of herself. Not, of course, that she expected to need that knowledge in Gregoria. There the watchwords would be elegance and propriety, at least until she found out what was going on behind the scenes and blew the lid off it.

The bell on the oven timer went off. She closed the closet door and returned to the kitchen. Over dinner she read through Gavin's file again. By midnight she was asleep and dreaming...about a dark-haired man with hazel eyes and an oddly tempting smile.

Chapter 2

Gavin was not smiling as he studied the report in his hand. A nervous aide stood beside his desk, waiting for his reaction. It was not long in coming.

"How did the leak happen?" Gavin demanded. "There's not a word in here to explain it."

"We have no information on that yet, sir," the thin young man said. "Our people are working on it."

The ambassador's mouth twisted skeptically. "Why doesn't that reassure me?"

"Beg pardon, sir?"

"Never mind. What counts is that the Russians have gotten wind of what's going on here in Gregoria and we can expect to have them on the scene shortly, if they aren't already."

Charles Paxton Landow III shifted from one foot to the other. He was twenty-six, a veteran of two years in the diplomatic corps, both of them spent in Gregoria. While his compatriots were dodging bullets in hardship posts, he had been free to indulge a passion for opera, fine wines and buxom blondes. That had suited him perfectly, until the arrival of the new ambassador, who had wasted no time making it clear that more was expected.

"Surely the Russians can't really be much of a threat," Landow ventured a shade smugly. "After all, sir, if there is any country on earth less likely to go communist than the United States itself, it must be Gregoria."

Gavin's piercing hazel eyes narrowed. "Why do you say that?"

The younger man smiled. He considered himself something of an expert on the subject and relished the opportunity to show off his knowledge. "Because this country is still living in the Middle Ages. They didn't even have electricity and plumbing until about fifty years ago, and since then hardly anything has changed. King Gregory is the last absolute monarch in the world, and his subjects are crazy about him."

Instead of responding to this information with the appreciation young Mr. Landow anticipated, Gavin gave him a long, level stare. "And that makes you think we've got nothing to worry about?"

"Well, I don't see where there would be any opportunity for insurgents to—"

"Let me fill you in on some of the harsher facts of life, Landow. His Highness's subjects aren't some bunch of dumb peasants tugging at their forelocks. They're fully aware of how different Gregoria is from the rest of the world, and some of them don't like it. The young people in particular watch television, listen to rock, and follow the latest fashions, just like everyone else. They want to be part of the modern age; in fact, they're insisting on it. King Gregory is fully aware of that. He sympathizes with them and he's determined to bring about change at a moderate, sensible pace. Provided, of course, that he gets the chance."

"Why wouldn't he?" Landow asked. He didn't care for being reprimanded by a man who had only been in the country a week, but he was smart enough not to show it. However much he might resent Gavin, the man was the new ambassador and, rumor had it, the fair-haired boy at State. It wouldn't do to get his hackles up.

Gavin hesitated. He had begun the meeting fully intending to take Landow into his confidence, but he wasn't so sure now. The younger man's smug, condescending attitude did not inspire trust. He made a mental note to see about shifting him over to a less delicate post. "Much as I'd enjoy discussing hypothetical problems, there really isn't time. I'd appreciate your checking on the arrangements for tomorrow's dinner. Get back to me when a selection of engagement gifts has been made. I'll make the final choice."

Surprised by the ambassador's sudden change of mood, Landow frowned. He realized that he had been dismissed, but the experience was so novel for him that he wasn't quite sure what to do. When he was still standing in front of the desk a moment later, Gavin looked up and said, "That will be all."

Landow nodded curtly, turned on his heel, and left the room. He shut the door a shade too loudly, but the gesture was lost on Gavin, who was already busy unlocking a desk drawer and removing a file from it.

Stamped across the file in neat letters were the words "Top Secret. Level AAA Security Clearance Required." Below that, in slightly smaller but still clearly legible type was the warning "Breach of security constitutes a felony offense punishable by prison sentence. Report all violations to the nearest security officer or F.B.I. agent."

Gavin flipped open the file, settled back in his chair, and began to read. It was not the first time he had gone through the material contained in the two dozen or so pages, but he read as carefully as though it had been. There was always the chance that he might have missed something or that another rereading would make clear a connection that he could use.

By nature he was a methodical man. Carrie had teased him about that. Her effervescent, impulsive character could not have been more at odds with his careful, meticulous approach to life. Yet for all of that, they could not have loved each other more. "Together we make a normal person," she had joked, without realizing how right she had been. Since her death, he had felt that a vital part of himself had been cut off, severed by a blow so clean that the wound didn't even bleed. It simply festered, month after month and year after year, as he struggled to come to terms with his grief.

Work had helped, and then there were the children. Without Jessie and David he didn't think he would have survived. Even with them, there had been nights when he lay awake, staring at the ceiling and wondering what the hell it was all about. In a world where a beautiful, loving woman could be cut down by insanity, anything at all could happen.

It was that constant awareness of the vagaries of fate that kept him more alert and aware than most other men. He knew his own reputation—for always being on top of a situation no matter how complex it might be—and he knew it was deserved. In the past, he had been entrusted with several extremely delicate missions and had carried each off well. But nothing had quite prepared him for the situation in Gregoria.

There could be real hell to pay.

Not in any casual meaning of that expression but in a terrifying, almost biblical way that, frankly, made his blood run cold. Armageddon. Few people even wanted to consider the possibility of it, but for those who like him understood the realities of nuclear armaments, it was a constant presence hanging over life; a dark, sulfurous cloud that nothing seemed able to banish.

Until now. Gavin leaned back in his chair, closed his eyes, and let his mind drift. If the recent discovery at

M.I.T. was on target and if a sufficient quantity of the new isotope could be found, then for the first time it would be possible to construct a truly effective defense against nuclear weapons that did not depend on mutually assured destruction. Humanity might actually be freed from the threat of nuclear war. His children could come to maturity in a world free of the mushroom cloud's specter.

It was almost too much to believe, yet he knew that the chance was there. If...if...if. So many things could yet go wrong, starting with securing the supply of xanium.

Almost from the moment of the M.I.T. breakthrough, a mad scramble had been underway to find where on earth the isotope might exist. Geological teams had spread out across the planet, searching deserts, mountain ranges, jungles, the ocean bottom, all in a frantic effort to find a source for what could be mankind's salvation.

All the teams had failed, except for one. Almost as an afterthought, two scientists had stopped off in Gregoria on their way back from Greece and Turkey. They made no secret of the fact that they had simply been curious about the ancient kingdom and seized the opportunity to spend a few days there. But they also hadn't completely forgotten the purpose of their trip, and almost as a lark, they had gathered and tested soil samples taken not far from the capital city. The results had stunned the small but unfortunately growing number of people who knew about them.

Gavin rose abruptly and walked over to the window overlooking the picturesque square. After a week of the same view, he was still far from used to it. How could he be when it was so different from anything he had seen before? Not even the ancient cities of Venice or Rome, where he had briefly served on special missions, could match the almost mystical quality of Gregoria, where time seemed if not to have stopped, then to have certainly slowed down.

Yet that was deceptive. In among the quaint horse-drawn wagons delivering produce to the buildings set around the square were an ample number of cars and motorbikes. Not enough to cause the traffic problems that existed in almost every other city, but sufficient to remind the viewer that Gregoria had at least one foot in the twentieth century—and the other stepping into the twenty-first.

Gavin sighed and ran a hand wearily through his thick chestnut hair. He had a full schedule that day, including another meeting with King Gregory, but he was also determined to spend some time with his children. Over breakfast, he had promised Jessie and David a trip to the royal zoo. It was a pledge he meant to keep while he still had the chance.

"I'll be back in a couple of hours," he told his secretary as he left the office. She nodded and gave him a smile that verged on warm, which for Virginia Witherspoon was saying a great deal. With twenty years of foreign service experience behind her, she harbored few illusions about the caliber of some diplomats. She had privately thought of Gavin's predecessor as "an ass," though her behavior toward him had always been the height of propriety.

She had viewed his replacement dubiously, until she realized that he was no soft-minded fob intent on enjoying a cushy posting. On the contrary, his keen mind missed nothing, and his sharp wit cut through the layers of bureaucratic mumbo-jumbo with practiced ease. He delighted her acerbic Boston soul and she didn't care who knew it. Barely forty-eight hours into his tenure, she had begun to favor Gavin with gracious approval that did not escape the notice of the rest of the embassy staff, who viewed the redoubtable Ms. Witherspoon as their bellwether. If she thought the new boss was someone to reckon with, the rest of them had better do the same.

Gavin responded to the respectful nods of several staff members as he strode down the corridor and out into the cool morning. The building that housed the American Embassy had been constructed in stages, beginning in the mid-1700s and ending some fifty years before. Oddly enough, its eclectic melange of styles blended, creating an agreeable if unusual whole. His own quarters were a spacious third-floor apartment stretching from the front of the building overlooking the square to the rear, where a secluded garden flourished. Jessie and David had loved it at first sight, which was a great relief to him, since he had feared their reaction to the move from Washington.

Trust children to adjust more readily than expected. He wished he could say the same for adults. While most of the embassy personnel were making the change from the easygoing style of his predecessor to his own hard-driving expectations, several were not. Besides Charles Landow, he could think of half a dozen others who would have to be shifted in position, if not reassigned altogether. Having to be bothered with personnel problems at such a time annoyed him, and he was frowning as he waved away his chauffeur and proceeded down the street.

Ordinarily, he would not have dreamed of doing such a thing. Even in the most seemingly safe capitals of Europe, an American diplomat who ventured out without proper security was a fool. He had long since become inured to that. But one of the side benefits of his posting to Gregoria was that he could be just a bit more relaxed about safety. Not because, as fools like Landow supposed, there was no possibility of trouble but because it suited his purpose to be seen as supremely confident.

Most of the other major embassies were also located in the square. He passed those of the French and British before coming to the stolidly ornate structure that housed the representatives of the Soviet Union. Two grim-faced guards outside the main entrance eyed him coldly as he passed. Deliberately he slowed his pace and glanced upward, in time to see a curtain flutter at the window he knew belonged to Karischenekov's office.

Good old Leonid. They had crossed swords before—in Paris and Bonn, not to mention Cairo. He respected the Russian, even deep down inside had some liking for him, and he suspected Karischenekov returned the sentiment. But that did not make them anything other than formidable opponents in a struggle where the stakes were so high that neither could afford to lose.

Gregory was another matter. Gavin smiled as he thought of the young king he was on his way to see. Landow had at least been right when he described him as the last absolute monarch; that much was true. But Gregory was far too intelligent not to wield his power subtly. There was nothing of the tyrant about him; on the other hand, he was firm in his beliefs and his requirements. Which Gavin hoped would make him easier to deal with in the long run.

The guards outside the royal palace had attracted the usual number of tourists come to photograph and admire. They milled about, talking in half a dozen languages, most of which Gavin understood. He caught speculation about the royal wedding, the chances of catching a glimpse of the king or Lady Althea, even gossip about whether or not it was a love match.

That last part amused him. Gregory had put off marrying until his early thirties simply because he was having too good a time to settle down. Not even the responsibilities of his position, which he accepted with a seriousness few suspected, had dissuaded him. Until he discovered that the charming little girl he had known all her life had suddenly bloomed into a radiantly beautiful young woman.

Gavin was no stranger to love; he had known it in full measure with Carrie and cherished the memory within his heart. But he was also aware of the terrible pain love could bring, and he hoped that whatever the outcome of his own dealings with Gregory, the man would never know anything like the agony that still had the power to wake him in a cold sweat, crying out against a reality that no amount of wishing would ever change.

She was gone, the woman he had loved more than his own life. He would gladly have died to protect her, but the chance had not been his. It was his fate to stay behind to look after their children and to serve his country—two responsibilities he took every bit as seriously as Gregory took his.

"His Highness will see you now," the majordomo said as a footman helped Gavin off with his coat. The antechamber to the royal office was a white and gold salon done in the style of Louis XV. It was rather too ornate to suit Gavin's taste, though he could appreciate the beauty and value of the magnificent Baroque ceiling mural and the chinoiserie furnishings.

The office beyond was much more to his liking. Large, perfectly proportioned, it was furnished much as a study in an English country house might have been. Which was hardly surprising when one considered that the royal house of Gregoria was by descent British, with a leavening of other nationalities added through marriages. The only surprising aspect of the remarkable line's history was that it should have happened at all. How the descendants of an inept crusader who had turned north instead of south had ended up as the oldest surviving royal dynasty in the world was a subject for another time.

"Thank you for coming, Mr. Ambassador," said the tall, slender man behind the desk as he rose and held out his hand. The gesture was graceful, as was the man himself. At thirty-two, King Gregory had a lean, lithe bearing that proclaimed him as much at ease on the sporting fields as in the halls of power. Side by side, he and Gavin were a study in contrasting types of virile appeal: the blunt-featured American exuding a sense of strength and determination versus the ruler guarded by layers of reserve and what the uninitiated might think of as arrogance.

Cool gray eyes missed nothing as they surveyed the newest addition to Gregoria's diplomatic community. Gavin inclined his head graciously. "Thank you for seeing me, Your Highness. I realize this is a very busy time for you."

Gregory's sudden smile stripped years from his age and made him look far more like the boy he had once been. "I had no idea arranging a wedding would be so complicated. Surely invasions have been planned more simply."

"I trust the Lady Althea is well."

The King's aquiline features softened further at the mention of his fiancée. "Very. She is taking it all with equanimity I cannot help but envy."

Gavin wasn't surprised. In the short time he had been in the kingdom, he had made it his business to learn as much about everyone who was anyone as he possibly could. Lady Althea, soon to be Her Royal Highness, consort of the King, definitely fell into that category. The research on her was as thorough as it was fascinating.

The male secretary hovering nearby was dismissed with a flick of the royal hand. Left alone, the two men settled on a leather couch in front of a large fireplace. Like most old buildings, the palace was less than adequately heated, making a fire welcomed on the cool spring morning.

"Coffee?" Gregory asked, indicating the silver service on the low table before them.

Gavin shook his head. "I'm trying to quit."

The king smiled. "One of the things I like best about Americans is your constant penchant for self-improvement. Perhaps because it's based on the belief that life really can be bettered."

"If you had to sum up the underlying philosophy of my country," Gavin said, "I suspect that would be it. Most of us are descendants of people who came seeking a better world. The dream hasn't been without its problems, but it's also turned out to have a good deal of truth to it."

"Shall we speak, then, of truth?" Gregory asked as he lifted the delicate porcelain cup to his lips. It looked somewhat incongruous in his large, capable hands, which were callused by long hours of sailing and riding. His eyes regarded Gavin steadily over the rim.

"I think, Your Highness, that we had better be as candid as possible with each other. There really is no time for dissembling."

"For you," Gregory reminded him. "Here time is regarded rather differently, less as something to be grasped and used, and more as an immutable facet of life that takes men where it will."

"You'd have a hard time convincing me that's really how you feel."

The king raised a regal eyebrow. "Even allowing for the differences between our cultures, Mr. Ambassador, it is hardly diplomatic to suggest I am attempting to mislead you."

"That's not what I meant. The tactic you're using is quite clear. You throw out a bit of bait and see if I take it. For instance, if I had bought the idea that you don't see the urgency of the present situation, you would have thought that both my government and myself lack any understanding of the realities here in Gregoria." Thinking of Landow, he added, "While I can see how you might have gotten that impression, I must tell you it is not accurate. At least not now."

Gregory put the cup down and leaned back, one long leg folded casually over the other. He was, as usual, dressed in the uniform of the Royal Hussars, a dark blue tunic worn over gray trousers and held at the waist by a leather belt with a silver clasp showing the seal of the house of Gregoria. The clothing was deceptively simple and unassuming; it suited the man.

"If there has been a change in your government's view of us, Mr. Ambassador, I would be glad to learn of it. Frankly, being regarded as something of a comic opera state is rather tedious."

"I won't pretend that wasn't the case. Gregoria has hardly been a high priority with us."

"You have, in fact, taken us for granted. Yet I must remind you that we have never formally aligned with the West. We have always been, and remain, staunchly neutral."

Which was precisely what was keeping the lights burning late at Foggy Bottom these days. Carefully, Gavin said, "Neutrality can be a very expensive, not to say dangerous, luxury, Your Highness."

Gregory smiled. "Why is it, Mr. Ambassador, that I'm getting the impression you are trying to warn me?"

"Because I am." Gavin took a deep breath before he continued. "We believe that there is going to be a serious attempt to undermine the government of this country, perhaps even to overthrow it, in order to secure the supply of xanium for the East Bloc. Should that happen, the effects on every Western nation will be extremely grave, but I doubt you personally will have to be concerned about them."

Only by the slightest flicker of his gray eyes did the king indicate that he had gotten the message. Another man might have expressed some dismay at learning that his position and possibly his life were in danger, but centuries of breeding did not permit such weakness. Gregory merely thought it over for a moment and shrugged. "I will do whatever I must to protect my people."

"Then may I suggest that a speedy accord with the United States—"

"My people," Gregory repeated with emphasis. "They are my primary concern, far more than my own well-being. I am not convinced that a treaty with your country would best serve their interests. Certainly one arrived at in haste would be regretted at leisure."

Gavin stifled an impulse to impatience. "I assure you, Your Highness, the United States wishes only what is best for both the Gregorian and American people."

Gregory held up a hand. "Spare me the platitudes, Mr. Ambassador. The United States wishes what is best for itself, as indeed it should. I, however, have no intention of allowing Gregoria to become a vassal state, not of your country or any other."

"As I said, Your Highness, neutrality can be both expensive and dangerous. To be blunt, in your circumstances I suspect it is also impossible."

"We shall see." The king rose and held out his hand. "Thank you again for stopping by, Mr. Ambassador. I'm sure we shall be speaking together a great deal in the coming days."

The audience was at an end. Gavin had to content himself with the fact that the lines of communication were still very much open. He left the palace with a new, wry appreciation of the man who led a medieval kingdom with a combination of ancient virtues and very modern pragmatism.

Chapter 3

I don't believe this place," Judith muttered under her breath as she put down her bag and glanced around the airport. A single runway led to a low stone building liberally wreathed in ivy and lichens that had been cleared away just enough to make room for a sign that read, Welcome to Gregoria. Customs and Immigration Inside. Next to it, a medieval round tower spouted radar antennae from its crenellated roof.

Low green hills wreathed in mist surrounded the airport. The ground was wet, indicating a recent shower, but the clouds had cleared, and the sunlight bouncing off the 727 behind her had a reassuringly cheery air. Which was just as well, since none of the passengers, including her, were in what could be described as a good mood.

Inside the Customs building, it was pandemonium. Three stoic-faced officials were attempting to deal with more than a hundred tired, irate passengers, most of whom were newspeople wanting only to get their equipment off-loaded, get to their hotels, and down several stiff drinks.

"It's a minicam," an exasperated young man in elaborately pressed khakis was saying. "A small camera, for taking pictures." He mimed a *click-click* with his fingers and in an aside to Judith said, "They do take pictures here, don't they?"

"I imagine so," she said quietly, offering her passport to another of the officials. Privately she thought the young man would do better if he showed more patience, but she didn't say so. The flight had been delayed leaving New York, and tempers were frayed.

"Te-le-vi-sion," the young man was saying, exaggerating each syllable with painful clarity. "Maybe I'm using the wrong language. What do they speak here, anyway?"

"English is fine, sir," the customs official said without inflection. "As is French, German, Spanish, or Italian. Whatever your preference."

Judith hid a smile as the young man, taken aback, had the grace to look embarrassed. She accepted the return of her passport, now stamped with a two-week visa bearing the visage of a fierce lion drawn straight from heraldry, and proceeded toward the exit where she hoped to find a cab.

A soft sound of dismay escaped her as she caught sight of the two rickety vehicles being fought over by several dozen of her colleagues. As one of the top correspondents of a national news magazine attempted to shove aside the host of the highest-rated morning news show, Judith closed her eyes and murmured a silent prayer for fortitude. She was a good traveler, inured to the difficulties of backwater living, but she had little tolerance for those in her profession who rarely ventured outside a major city, and then only with cumbersome retinues that required constant care and feeding. Not one of those subscribing to the belief that a shortage of ice for drinks was a major hardship and a lack of overnight laundry facilities too much to bear, she was caught between amusement and annoyance.

Amusement won, and before she could stop herself, she laughed. The sound caught the attention of a grizzled old man standing off to one side, also observing the scene. He tilted his head in her direction and grinned. "Very hard for them, no? Two cabs, too many people. What to do?"

"Turn the airport into a hotel?" Judith suggested.

The old man spread his worn hands. "Alas, there is no bar, and the facilities are, shall we say, primitive. I doubt any of these august personages would be satisfied."

"I suspect you're right." She offered her hand and he accepted it gravely, bowing with old-world courtliness. "I'm Judith Fairchild. I work for a television network in the United States, and I'm here to cover the wedding of His Royal Highness and Lady Althea Desiree."

The old man's face lit in a beatific smile. "Our king has chosen well. She is a beautiful flower who will bear him many sons."

If Judith was taken aback by so chauvinistic a view, she didn't show it. Years of tromping all over the world had given her respect and tolerance for the vast range of human attitudes. "I'm sure she will," she murmured politely. "Tell me, is there any other way into the city besides these two taxis?" She tilted her head toward the disreputable vehicles, still being fought over as their drivers stood by, smiling benignly.

"Yes," the old man acknowledged, "but I fear a lovely lady such as you might not find it suitable."

Judith's smile broadened. "I assure you, sir, that I would find anything appropriate that could get me to my hotel."

"Even that?" he asked with a twinkle in his old black eyes.

Following the direction of his hand, Judith noticed the sturdy wagon drawn up behind the cabs with a patient old nag calmly munching out of an oat bag. Various boxes and crates bearing air freight labels from all over Europe were stacked in the wagon.

"I have the honor to serve at the palace," the old man explained. "My name is Sebastian de la Croix. For generations my family has helped to supply the royal kitchens by purveying goods from beyond our borders. Twice a week I come to the airport to collect the shipments."

"How fortunate for me that you do," Judith said. "If you wouldn't mind giving me a lift, I would greatly appreciate it."

Sebastian assured her that it was his pleasure to serve such a delightful guest to his country. He refused her help to lift her luggage into the wagon and handed her up onto the wooden seat with a flourish that could only be described as courtly.

Under the bemused gazes of her fellow correspondents, who were still struggling to secure their own transportation, the wagon departed at a sedate but steady gait. "Esmerelda is a good horse," Sebastian said of the nag. "No longer young, but she knows her business. I could stay home in bed and she would still be here to meet the planes."

"Has there been an airport here for very long?" Judith asked. She had to hold on to the side of the wagon to keep her balance, but she nonetheless found the ride quite agreeable. It had warmed up slightly, enough for her to loosen her suede jacket. A fresh breeze redolent of the sea fluttered her blond hair and added a dash of color to cheeks made pale by the long flight.

"The airstrip was built fifteen years ago," Sebastian told her. "It was smaller then and not paved, so only a few planes could land here. Last year it was expanded so that the big jets could come."

"The buildings next to it look very old."

The old man chuckled softly. "Like most things here in Gregoria. The tower was built by the illustrious King Gregory the First, founder of the royal house. It has stood for some eight hundred years, yet it continues to serve a purpose. As for the other, it was originally the home of monks who lived here in the sixteenth century.'' He laughed again. ''Who knows what such holy men would make of its present use.''

''Did people object to the airport being built?'' Judith asked. She had heard that change came very slowly in Gregoria, and not without opposition.

Sebastian cast her a look from the corner of his eye. ''There might have been a few who did so, but they have accepted what was done.'' Almost as an aside, he added, ''King Gregory knows how to make such things palatable.''

She took that to mean that the king knew how to handle those of his subjects who wanted to cling to the past while still moving his country resolutely into the future. That didn't accord with the image she had of him as a high-living playboy who thought only of his own pleasures.

Which was fine. Judith liked surprises; in fact, she thrived on them. They were the stuff that turned an ordinary story into a blockbuster. If there were surprises in Gregoria, she meant to unearth them.

At the thought of doing so, a smile played across her generous mouth. Sebastian saw it and asked, ''Something pleases you?''

''The, uh, countryside. It's very beautiful.''

He nodded as though praise of his native land was no oddity to him. ''We are near the foothills of the Thessely mountains. It is said that in the old days, gods played there and their golden essence still lingers."

"What a lovely idea. Very poetic."

"Of course," her new-found friend added, "it is also said that they are the result of geological upheavals during the Triassic era."

Judith sputtered but regained her composure swiftly. "Which do you believe?"

Sebastian shrugged. "Both, of course."

"That's a rare ability."

"It is part of being Gregorian," he said, "as you will discover should you remain here long enough. We accept all possibilities, deny nothing, and pick and choose that which is pleasant to us."

"And that which is not?"

"We ignore."

"I don't know," Judith said, shaking her head. "There's a great deal in this world that can't simply be brushed aside because it's inconvenient or unpleasant."

"On the other hand, a great deal too much attention is paid to such things instead of to what really matters." Without pausing for breath, he added, "You are not married."

"No," Judith felt compelled to say, though it hadn't really been a question.

"Is there a man in your life?"

"No again, at least not at the moment."

Sebastian sighed deeply, and it seemed that the old nag sighed with him. "It is so often the way. A beautiful woman who should be surrounded by the love of her husband and children is instead alone. And why, I ask you, simply so you can do a job, earn money, and grow old by yourself?''

"Work can be as important to a woman as it is to a man," she said. "I get a great deal of satisfaction from mine." Not enough to stop her from too often wanting what the old man was talking about, but she wasn't going to admit that to a stranger, however charming he might be.

Nonetheless, a hint of her sadness must have reached Sebastian for he gave her a gentle smile. "All things that are meant to be eventually come."

"That sounds very fatalistic."

"I suppose it is. Remember, here in Gregoria we stand on the crossroads between the great faiths of both East and West. We've had our share of mystics and holy men. Perhaps while you are here you will visit the caves outside the city where hermits once lived."

"Perhaps," Judith said, though she thought it unlikely. She would be far too concerned with the events of the present day to concern herself much with the past.

The rest of the way into town, she and Sebastian enjoyed an amicable silence that was broken only when he pulled up in front of the Hotel Royale and Judith's mouth fell open. She was looking at architecture run amok. Uncounted towers, each more elaborate than the last, rose from a base that somehow managed to resemble the great pyramid of Cheops. Sprouting from it in all directions were wings that appeared taken from Versailles, various English country houses, and the White House. The whole was a startling, oddly whimsical concoction which, as she promptly said, "looks like something Mad King Ludwig of Bavaria might have built."

Far from being offended by her blunt assessment of the gingerbread fantasia perched before them, Sebastian grinned. "Indeed, miss, it was built by a monarch, King Gregory the Nineteenth, to celebrate his marriage to the Princess Wilheminia Fredericka in 1872. The king was a devoted patron of architecture in all its many forms."

"Oh...that explains it." Their eyes met—hers slightly glazed, his twinkling—and despite her best resolve, Judith burst out laughing. "I'm sorry, it's just that I've never seen such...an ecletic structure."

"Further delights await you inside."

As indeed they did. The ornately uniformed footman—bell boy simply didn't describe him—who carried her luggage into the lobby showed no surprise at her method of arrival. On the contrary, he displayed a degree of deference toward Sebastian that made Judith think that either the elderly were treated with far greater respect in Gregoria than was the case in many other countries or her new friend's position at the palace wrapped him in the aura of power by association. Whichever, the footman was propriety itself, as was the receptionist in black tie and swallow's tails who inclined his head gravely when she gave her name and ruffled through a stack of cards to find her reservation.

"Ah, yes, Miss Fairchild, here we are. You'll be staying with us for ten days?"

"That's right."

"Here for the wedding?"

She nodded but made no effort to prolong the conversation. Jet travel had never agreed with her, despite all her experience with it. She was tired, gritty, and wanted only to retire to her room for a much-needed shower and nap.

"If there is anything you require," the desk clerk said, "you have only to pull the velvet rope by the bed. That will summon a servant."

"There are no telephones in the rooms?"

"But of course, you may call for room service if you prefer." He said that in such a way as to indicate that if she insisted on making use of such newfangled devices, that was her privilege.

As it was, Judith spent some fifteen minutes searching for the telephone, finding it eventually in a marble and mahogany table beside the carved four-poster bed that dominated her room. With a sigh of relief, she picked up the receiver and placed a call to Sam Wexman in New York. She had expected to have to wait for perhaps several hours before the call could go through, but to her surprise she was connected immediately. The Gregorians might not approve of telephones, but they knew how to use them efficiently.

"How's it going?" Sam demanded as soon as he heard her voice. "Anything happening?"

Judith wiggled her way out of her shoes and lay back on the bed, her head propped up by a generous goose-down pillow that felt like sheer heaven. "Nothing much. I just got in and thought I'd put my feet up for a few hours before I start to sniff around."

"Dave called in. The crew's still stuck in Paris."

Her film crew, whom she had worked with several times in the past, had taken a different flight and been delayed in the French capital by a thick fog. "I'll bet they're all broken up about that."

"I told him to get his butt down there tomorrow if he has to walk."

Good old Sam. No mere act of God was going to get in the way of his schedule. "I want you on the air with your first reports no later than Wednesday. Got that?"

"Sure, sure, just don't expect me to sound thrilled about cutesy interviews with Their Highnesses."

"You'll be lucky if you can get near them. Word has it that Gregory is too busy to fool with the media and Lady Althea is being kept behind closed doors."

"Wonder why that is," Judith said, more to herself than to Sam. Maybe there was something there that bore looking into.

"That's for you to find out. Get some rest and then get to it."

"Rest first? You're getting soft, Sam."

"You should live so long. Anything on the other matter we discussed?"

They had agreed in advance that there would be no direct references over the telephone to Gavin Penderast or the M.I.T. discovery. Not that either of them really thought they might be overheard; it just didn't hurt to be cautious.

"No, but . . . hold on a minute." She picked up an embossed envelope that had been waiting on the bedside table when she arrived and glanced at it. "There's something here from the embassy." Opening it quickly, she scanned the neatly scripted card inside. "Seems I'm invited to a reception there tonight."

"How nice."

"Actually, it will probably be boring as hell."

"But you'll go anyway?"

"I'd much rather stay in, wash my hair, and catch up on my research."

"Judith . . ."

"Just kidding, Sam. Of course I'll go. With all the taxes I pay, you think I'd pass up an opportunity to get some of them back in caviar and champagne?"

Sam chuckled. "I guess not."

They talked a few minutes longer about various other stories that were in the works. Since Judith wasn't involved in them directly, there was no reason for the discussion except that it reconfirmed her status as the top runner for the anchor spot. Should she get it, she would be expected to coordinate all daily news coverage. Sam apparently thought it useful to get her accustomed to that right off the bat.

Which should have made her feel good, except that she really was tired, and more than that, her present assignment had her more preoccupied than usual. There were still too many unknowns about it, too many imponderables. Not the least of which was the chance that she really was on a wild goose chase.

If that was the case, she would just as soon find out right away. Gavin Penderast would undoubtedly be at the reception, since he was hosting it. She intended to use the opportunity to meet him and judge for herself whether Sam's suspicions had any basis in fact.

Which meant that all her faculties had to be razor-sharp. Easier said than done, though a quick snooze as soon as she got off the phone helped. She awoke precisely forty-five minutes later and lay for a moment staring up at the embroidered canopy above the bed before she swung her long legs over the side and headed for the bathroom. The ability to fall asleep quickly and wake as readily was a tremendous asset in her line of work. Nonetheless, she needed the cold shower she subjected herself to, gritting her teeth and remaining under it until the last of the travel-induced cobwebs was blown from her mind.

Only when she had fumbled her way into the thick terry cloth robe provided by the hotel and tied the belt snugly around her slender waist did she take proper notice of the bathroom. Shaking her head in sheer amazement that so much gilt and marble could be crammed into a single space, she wiped the steam from the mirror and began speedily to dry and style her hair.

An hour later she left the hotel and took a taxi the short distance to the American Embassy. A solemn-faced Marine guard checked her invitation before admitting her. She passed through the entry hall decorated with portraits of Washington and Lincoln, as well as the current president.

Malcolm Harrison gazed down at her benevolently. Silver-haired, crinkly-eyed, he had been an extremely successful businessman before rallying the voters with a pledge to make the country competitive again. Barely six months in office, he was still something of an unknown quantity. Judith instinctively distrusted him, not because of anything to do with the man himself but because as a reporter she had to be skeptical of all those who aspired to power. Yet the several times she had interviewed him, she had found him both candid and charming—a rare combination that she couldn't help but wonder would also be present in the man he had chosen as his newest ambassador.

Which brought her to the subject of Gavin Penderast. There was a receiving line directly inside the ballroom. Judith joined it, oblivious to the admiring glances she received from many of the other guests, particularly the men. She knew she looked good but saw nothing especially noteworthy about that. Her celebrity status guaranteed her a certain amount of attention, which she had become adroit at ignoring.

Several people were still ahead of her on the line when she caught sight of Penderast. Any idea she might have had that the man wouldn't live up to his advance billing died at that instant. If anything, he looked even more ruggedly handsome and unmistakably virile than she had been led to expect. It took all her considerable self-control to remind herself that she was there to do a job, not to stare in awestruck admiration at what could easily pass for a Greek god.

Judging by the behavior of the other women, she was far from the only one to be so affected. Yet the men showed no sign of resentment. On the contrary, there was a back-slapping bonhomie that belied the formality of the occasion.

The ambassador was laughing at some sally from one of the men when his eyes met Judith's. A dark slash of eyebrow rose as he studied her with a scrutiny that under any circumstances would be considered so intense as to be rude. Yet she took no offense, knowing that she was doing exactly the same to him.

A shiver of recognition moved through her, all out of keeping with her impersonal acquaintance with this man. The line moved forward. Her hand touched his, warm flesh against silken skin. She jumped slightly, as did he. Electricity ran between them; potent, primeval, the force of life itself.

"Miss Fairchild." His voice was deep, a caress running over and through her. His eyes remained intent, slightly narrowed, as though he was as affected as she by the spark they struck on each other.

"Mr. Ambassador." She knew she should say something else, make some polite social chitchat, but the effort was beyond her. All she could think of was that her neat, organized world had suddenly spun out of control. As though a comet had hurled out of the farthest reaches of space to illuminate a previously dark stretch of sky.

Their hands still touching, she took in the smallest nuances of his appearance, the hard slash of his mouth, the cleft in his chin, the tiny scar above his right eye, with a fascination she would previously have reserved for a great painting or statue. She was being rude and foolish, but she could not help herself.

Her lips parted soundlessly and she felt the touch of his eyes falling to them. The broad chest beneath his elegantly tailored evening clothes rose sharply. Their eyes met again, and in a flash she knew exactly what he was thinking.

Chapter 4

He wanted to take her to bed. To strip her naked, lay her down, and possess her, utterly and completely. That unbridled male instinct drummed through Gavin's blood, hardening his body explicitly. It was all he could manage not to pull her into his arms, lift her off her feet, and carry her away.

Which was ridiculous. He wasn't some horny caveman, for God's sake! He was an ambassador, the representative of his country. Moreover, he was a father and a widower; that last part made the sudden onslaught of desire all the more shocking. He had had women since Carrie's death, but infrequently and reluctantly, giving in only when simple physical need became too great to bear. This was different.

Without understanding how, he sensed that the slender, pale woman before him could wreak havoc with his life, if he let her. And perhaps even if he didn't. Carefully, with all the caution of his intrinsically wary nature, he studied her. She looked taller than she did on the television screen; he had seen her during a stopover in New York on his way to Gregoria and had been impressed by her solid professionalism, which mingled with a degree of warmth that came across well on camera.

In person, it was a different story. He told himself that he was imagining it, but she seemed to radiate a kind of sexual tension at odds with her elegant appearance and self-contained manner. The black dress she wore was simple to the point of austerity. Far from being low-cut as were the gowns of many of the other women, it had a high collar that completely covered her throat. A gold chain with a heart-shaped locket stood out against the dark fabric.

Her arms and shoulders were bare, revealing skin that glowed with the sheen of satin. His fingers curled inward as he had to consciously resist the impulse to determine for himself if she was as soft as she looked. The dress lightly skimmed her breasts, clung gently to her narrow waist, and fell over her hips to the tops of black evening shoes. Except for the locket, she wore no jewelry other than a watch on a plain black band. Her hair, awash with light from the crystal chandeliers, was as simply styled as everything else about her.

Beside her, every other woman in the reception hall looked overblown. Which wasn't fair, Gavin realized the moment the thought occurred to him. How could any woman be expected to compete with the vision who stared back at him with unflinching blue eyes thickly fringed by dark lashes, whose soft, full mouth parted in the slightest of smiles when he at last released her hand.

Aware that he was perilously close to breaching diplomatic etiquette, Gavin managed a slight, formal nod of his head. "Miss Fairchild, how nice of you to attend. We weren't sure you would make it, since you arrived only this afternoon."

For a moment, Judith heard only the deep, caressing timbre of his voice; the words themselves meant nothing until she took a deep breath and managed, through sheer force of will, to at least partially clear her head. "Are you always so up-to-date on the movements of journalists, Mr. Ambassador?"

"Very little goes on in Gregoria without someone commenting on it," he told her. A twinkle appeared in his hazel eyes as he added, "Besides, Sebastian also delivers goods to the embassy."

Judith, who normally was as prickly as any other reporter about the rights of the media, found herself smiling. "I should have guessed it was something like that. He's quite gregarious."

He cast her a quick look she couldn't decipher, not that she really had a chance. An aide was trying to subtly prod her on while at the same time turning the ambassador's attention to the next person in the receiving line.

The ambassador resisted the pressure long enough to say, "There will be dancing after dinner, Miss Fairchild. Perhaps you would be good enough to save me a waltz?"

There was no opportunity to respond as the line moved on, but the smile he gave her expressed confidence that she would accede to his request, as did the frosty glare of the matron who had been impatiently waiting behind her. Under other circumstances, Judith would have found the situation humorous. As it was, she was pensive as she strolled into the gallery where drinks and hors d'oeuvres were being served. Deliberately, she forced herself to think of the job at hand.

With the exception of the startling physical attraction between them—which she shied away from recalling too graphically—Ambassador Penderast was everything she had expected. He lived up to the dossier that described a man of rare ability and drive, a man on the fast track at the State Department, trusted by other men who saw the world without illusion and were ruthless in their pragmatism.

Again she came back to the question she had posed to Sam Wexman: If Ambassador Penderast was such hot stuff, what was he doing in Gregoria?

Her pulse quickened slightly, though there was no outward sign of her excitement. More and more she was coming to think that there really was a story here, a big one that could seal her own career aspirations. If she was right, nothing was going to stop her from getting it, especially not a capricious surge of hormones.

"Champagne, madam?" a waiter inquired as he proffered a silver tray upon which rested tulip-shaped goblets.

Judith accepted one and sipped it absently as she surveyed the crowd. There was the usual assortment for such occasions: diplomats, business people, a handful of representatives from the arts, and the few who couldn't quite be pegged and might be anything from mere hangers-on to agents of various governments or private interests.

About a dozen or so were journalists like her, and among them she recognized Jim West, the young man from the airport. He saw her at the same time and raised his glass in acknowledgment before making his way through the crowd to her side.

"Some party," he said as he looked her over with that expression of frankly sexual approval that certain men imagine to be so flattering. "I saw that little trick you pulled at the airport. Nice work."

"I was glad to be offered a lift, Mr...?"

"West, Jim West." He paused for a moment, as though expecting her to recognize his name. When she did not, his smile faded slightly. "NBC. Before that I was with Reuters. Put in some time in Central America. Pretty rough there. Nothing like it, though, living in the bush, relying on your wits. Not like this place." He glanced around disparagingly.

Young men, Judith decided, who had chosen journalism as a career should resist the temptation to present themselves as the newest incarnation of Ernest Hemingway. Particularly when they were so defensive about their self-importance.

Jim West looked to be about twenty-eight, which might have meant something except she was willing to bet that they had been easy years, his allusion to Central America notwithstanding. His slightly plump face had the smooth, untroubled look of those for whom physical comfort and emotional complacency is a birthright. Yet his smallish eyes were sharp enough to suggest that he was no stranger to the kind of ambition that roots in envy. He wanted to make something of himself, did Jim West. The world—and television—being what they were, he might just do it.

All this passed through Judith's mind in an instant. She was accustomed to sizing people up quickly; in her line of work that was a necessity. Though she was never arrogant about her judgments, experience had taught her that she was rarely wrong. Yet she was by nature polite and, more than that, compassionate. She sensed that it was important for West to be seen talking with a woman he regarded as desirable. For a few moments, she would indulge him.

"What brings you to Gregoria, Mr. West?" she asked before taking another sip of her champagne.

Her tone conveyed only the most superficial interest, but that passed blithely over his head. "The wedding, of course, which I don't mind telling you I wasn't thrilled to get stuck with. I'm working on a couple of stories right now that are really hot. I mean, big stuff."

"Hmmm," Judith murmured, then plucked a stuffed grape leaf off a passing tray and nibbled on it. If she had a dollar for every reporter who had bragged to her about big stories in the works, she could have bought a vineyard of grape leaves.

Sensing that he was losing his audience, West pressed on. "I'm not always going to be just another correspondent for the network, you know. No, sir, I've got my cap set a whole lot higher than that. And I hear you do, too." Meaningfully, he added, "So maybe we ought to get to know each other better."

"You really ought to try these," she said before popping the last of the grape leaf into her mouth. "They're terrific."

He drew back slightly. "I'm not crazy about foreign food."

"That must be quite a problem then, with all the traveling you do."

Why was she feeding him lines, Judith wondered, when her boredom quotient was low and West was closing in on it fast? If she wasn't careful, she'd be stuck with him as her partner at dinner.

"I do all right," he assured her. "You'd be surprised what good old American dollars can still accomplish. I could give you a few tips...."

"Thanks, but if you'll excuse me, I really need to freshen up."

"You look fine to me."

If there was one thing Judith couldn't stand, it was a man who wouldn't take a hint. A flash of what one perceptive reviewer had dubbed her "killer frost" crept into her voice. "How nice, but I think I'm the best judge of that."

West scowled but made no further effort to detain her, which was just as well, since she was feeling less patient than usual. In the ladies' room—yet another fantasia in gilt and marble—she ran cold water on her wrists in an effort to throw off the lingering blanket of fatigue. Around her, gloriously gowned and bejeweled women were chattering away in half a dozen languages, filling the air with puffs of Arpege and Gauloises, their shrill laughter bouncing off the brocaded walls.

More than a few eyed her assessingly, but Judith remained oblivious to their stares. Her encounter with Jim West had reminded her of how oddly she had reacted to Gavin Penderast. Granted, the contrast between the two men was enormous, but it did not fully explain the difference in her own responses. Deep inside, Judith prided herself on always being in firm control of her emotions. It was a skill won at high price and therefore appropriately valued. Any threat to that control frightened her.

Not that she was afraid of Gavin Penderast. The mere idea was ludicrous. He was only a man, better-looking than most, with a rare sense of strength and determination, but still only a man. And she was hardly some schoolgirl in the throes of a crush.

Which did not explain why, when she caught sight of him again across the crowded gallery, her heart quickened and she momentarily forgot to breathe. She had a fortuitous encounter just then when a tall, blond man in the uniform of the Royal Hussars introduced himself to her.

"Louis, Duke of Montfort," he said with a smile that suggested he didn't take that grandiose title too seriously. "I've learned that if one waits at these things to be properly presented, it never happens. So I thought I'd do the job myself."

"I'm glad you did," Judith said frankly. She judged him to be about thirty-five, aristocratic of bearing, and good-looking without being overly impressed by the fact. He bore a slight resemblance to pictures she had seen of King Gregory, which she mentioned.

"My cousin," he said. "We grew up together. Allow me to take you in to dinner, and I'll tell you all sorts of delicious palace gossip."

Judith doubted very much that he would do any such thing, but she still agreed, finding his company a welcome distraction from her preoccupation with the ambassador. With a smile, she allowed Louis to place her hand on his arm and escort her into the banquet room. Chatting with him, she did not notice the interested looks they got, as together they made a dazzling couple.

Gavin, on the other hand, did notice. Very little about the blond reporter escaped him. He had seen her talking to Jim West, seen her disappear briefly and then return to be zeroed in on by Montfort. Not that he could blame him. Judith was not only a beautiful and delightful companion; she also had a way about her that suggested she wasn't impressed by externalities but sought instead for the inner man. Nothing could be more flattering, though he doubted that she realized it.

Montfort certainly did, and was lapping it up, not unlike the proverbial cat with a saucer of cream. Except that this cat was more a tiger than a tabby and clearly had hunting in mind. Gavin frowned, disconcerting the pigeon-chested matron seated next to him, who had imagined him enthralled by her talk of fashionable resorts and shopping sprees. He had other plans for Judith, Montfort and his own reservations notwithstanding.

Shortly after dessert, the company began adjourning to the ballroom, where Gregoria's Royal Orchestra, specially hired for the occasion, was playing. One thing that could be said for diplomatic parties was that the people who attended them knew what was expected of them. There was none of the awkward standing around that occurred in other such situations where couples waited for someone else to be first on the dance floor. Instead, after Gavin had led out the wife of the senior member of the Gregorian Parliament, others followed smoothly, and by the time the second dance was underway, the ballroom floor was pleasantly crowded.

Judith stood off to one side, watching the proceedings and trying dutifully to put names to faces for future reference. As the ranking member of the royal family, Louis was required to perform numerous duty dances. His mask of politeness slipped just far enough for him to shoot Judith a wry glance as he whirled past with a substantial matron who fairly gushed in his arms.

Judith coughed lightly to cover her laugh. She drifted around the edges of the room, careful to avoid Jim West, who, in any case, appeared not to be dancing. The ambassador, on the other hand, was, and seemed to be doing an excellent job of it. But then in his line of work he undoubtedly had a great deal of experience carrying out such duties.

Drawn up short by such unaccustomed acerbity, Judith silently admitted that any attempt to typecast him as a dilettante would be utterly off target. Even if she hadn't read the dossier on him, she would have sensed that he was far more than a charmer adept at social niceties. Which might be an interesting point to raise with him if and when she got the chance.

It came sooner than she had expected. When he had asked her to save him a waltz, she had only half thought he was serious. But barely had he completed the last of his duty dances before he was at her side.

"Not dancing?" he asked with a smile.

Some imp of mischief inspired her to be flirtatious. "Oh, I've been waiting for you."

"I'll pretend to believe that," he said, taking her hand without further ado.

Judith was not used to quite such assertive men. Rather than make a scene, she allowed herself to be led onto the dance floor, but her hackles were up, and he seemed to sense that as he drew her into his arms.

"I'm not usually so peremptory," he said.

"*I'll* pretend to believe *that*."

They looked at each other challengingly for a moment, then abruptly relaxed and laughed. "Something tells me we're well matched," he said, not without a hint of chagrin.

She did not respond directly, but the wariness that darkened her eyes spoke volumes. Gavin stifled a sigh. There was a certain irony in being intensely drawn to a woman for the first time since Carrie, and to have her as cautious of the attraction as he was himself.

"I think," Judith murmured as they moved together gracefully to the strains of the waltz, "that I should make something clear."

Though he suspected what she was about to say, Gavin asked, "What's that?"

"I make it a hard and fast rule never to get personally involved with someone who's part of my work."

"What's that got to do with me, or, more to the point, with us?"

"There is no us," she said pointedly, "nor is there going to be. You're part of this assignment. I would like to interview you."

Gavin frowned slightly. "You're here to cover the royal wedding. I've got nothing to do with that."

"Correction. I'm here to cover the situation in Gregoria, of which the wedding is only a part." Deliberately, she met his eyes as she added, "My guess is a very small part."

"I doubt if His Royal Highness and Lady Althea would agree," Gavin said smoothly even as his mind slipped into high gear. The lovely woman flowing so naturally against him knew something. He wasn't sure

what or how, but she was sending an unmistakable
signal that she believed she was on to a major story.
And if she was, he had better find out where she stood,
fast.

"One of the things I'd like to talk with you about,"
she was saying, "is how you happened to be sent to
Gregoria. It seems like quite a backwater for a man
with your credentials."

Worse and worse, Gavin thought. She might as well
have raised a red flag in front of him. Still, he smiled
imperturbably. "That's hardly flattering to our
hosts."

Her full mouth tightened, fair warning to him that
she was running out of patience. "We can spar like
this as long as you like, Mr. Ambassador, but the plain
fact of the matter is that I've got questions that demand answers. If I can't get them from you, I'm going
to be asking them elsewhere."

His hazel eyes flashed ominously. "That sounds
suspiciously like a threat."

"You can take it any way you wish." Normally, it
didn't bother Judith in the least to be so tough, but
just then she was having trouble dealing with it. The
woman in her was drawn almost irresistably to him;
with very little effort she could find herself surrender-
ing to his compelling masculinity. But the professional side of her nature would not permit it. She
straightened her back, all the while vividly aware of
the warm press of his hand against her bare skin, and
met his gaze unflinchingly.

The tiniest of smiles lifted the corners of his hard mouth. "All right, Miss Fairchild. May I suggest that you stay on after the other guests have left? We'll have a drink together and talk about Gregoria."

Careful not to show how pleased she was by her victory, Judith nodded. "That will be fine."

She was very confident, Gavin thought when he reluctantly allowed Montfort to claim the next dance and went to have a word with his new aide, a considerably more astute young man who had just replaced Landow. But then she had no monopoly on confidence. His smile held a predatory gleam as he considered what he would say to her when they were alone. And what he would do.

Chapter 5

The study where Judith sat was paneled in mahogany and furnished with pieces any museum would have envied. Red velvet drapes were drawn across the floor-to-ceiling windows. A lamp on the desk cast shadows over the ranks of leather-bound books covering the walls. Over the fireplace, in which a cheerful blaze flickered, hung a landscape that Judith had inspected earlier and confirmed to be a Wylie.

She had been brought to the study by an elderly butler who, after lighting the fire and pouring her a brandy, had withdrawn silently, shutting the double doors behind him. That had been half an hour ago. She had admired the room and finished the brandy; now she was bored.

Waiting was not her long suit. She freely admitted her own impatience and did her best to curb it. That wasn't always easy, but over the years she had learned to assume an air of unconcern that fooled most people.

It didn't work with Gavin. The moment he entered the study, he felt her tension. Going over to the cart that held an array of bottles, he reached for the brandy before looking at her. "Care for another?"

She shook her head. "One's my limit."

A cautious woman, he thought, who was aware of her own capacity and disciplined enough to stick to it. Having half filled a snifter with the amber liquid, he carried it with him to the couch and sat down beside her. "I'm sorry to keep you waiting."

"That's quite all right. I'm aware that you have many demands on your time."

"Actually, I would have been here sooner except that one of my children had a nightmare. The nurse had a standing order to call me whenever that happens."

"I see...." Judith stumbled over the personal revelation. For one of the few times in her life she was uncertain of what to say. "Do they...that is...are nightmares frequently a problem?"

"Less than they used to be. Jessie has a bad cold right now, and that makes her more susceptible. But after Carrie, my wife, was killed, Jessie didn't sleep a night through for at least six months. She was there when it happened, you see, and unlike Davey, she was old enough to remember."

"Davey, your son, he was only a few months old, wasn't he?"

"Do you have an exceptionally good memory, or did you read up on me before coming over here?"

Judith took a deep breath and looked into the fire. He had caught her neatly. She had to admire his technique even as she couldn't help but resent it. "The latter. I saw a dossier on you that mentioned your wife's death."

"Her murder. I've never been able to think of it simply as a death."

"I'm sorry." Judith spoke very softly, but she knew he heard the words. The eyes he turned on her were filled with the shadows of torment, yet also with great strength. He had lived through a tragedy that would have destroyed many other men. Instead he had been tempered by it to the finest of steels. That she couldn't help but admire.

"It was a long time ago," he said before taking a long swallow of his brandy that granted nothing to the rare old vintage except its ability to dull pain. "At any rate, that's not what we're here to talk about." He stiffened suddenly. "Is it?"

"No," Judith hastened to assure him. Undoubtedly he had been approached by reporters in the past who wanted to rake over the tragedy. She was appalled that he would even think she might be another of them. "I want to talk about xanium."

A muscle flexed in his jaw. He raised a hand to pull his tie loose and undo the top button of his shirt. "Mind if I get comfortable?"

Judith suppressed a smile. If she hadn't been quite so adept at what she did, she wouldn't have been sure that the dart had struck home. As it was, she knew she had a direct hit.

"I seem to remember reading about something called xanium recently," he said.

"I'm sure you do."

"A newspaper article, perhaps."

"More likely a government report. Do you think we could get down to brass tacks, Mr. Ambassador?"

"I don't know about that, Miss Fairchild. I'm rather enjoying things the way they are." That was true, though it surprised him. She presented quite a problem to him, yet if he could have waved his hand and made her disappear, he wouldn't have done it. Beyond the sheer physical desire that had struck him so forcibly—and continued to simmer just below the surface—there was something about her that fascinated him. A mixture of strength, tenacity, and intelligence he could not help but admire.

Which did not mean that he could afford to relax his guard with her for even an instant.

He took another sip of his brandy, crossed one long leg over the other and regarded her steadily. "Suppose you tell me what it is you think you know."

She smiled. "That's like asking me to show my hand at poker before I've won the pot."

"Do you play poker, Miss Fairchild?"

"I've been known to."

"Interesting. We have a friendly little game here at the embassy every once in a while. You'd be welcome to sit in."

"That would depend on the stakes, Mr. Ambassador."

"Please, call me Gavin."

She inclined her head in tacit agreement. "And I'm Judith."

"Would I be right to guess that no one has ever called you Judy?"

The dimples that appeared at the corners of her mouth when her smile deepened entranced him. "Not twice."

He laughed, a deep, rich sound that sparked an answering curl of warmth inside her. "I can see how that would be. Diminutives don't suit you."

"Dare I ask what that means?"

"Only that you're a woman to be reckoned with, Judith."

"How fortunate that you've already realized that, Gavin." She spoke steadily enough, though she felt anything but. Their banter had taken an unexpectedly intimate turn that she found oddly exhilarating, even as she told herself that she had to get the conversation back on track. Ambassador Penderast— Gavin—was a highly seductive man, in all sorts of ways. He appealed to her mind as well as her senses, a double-pronged attack of which she was instinctively wary.

"Suppose," she said, "that you tell me why a man of your background has been sent to Gregoria."

"I'm surprised you should have to ask. The strategic importance of Gregoria is obvious, given its location between East and West."

"Successive administrations have managed to overlook that geographical fluke."

"Perhaps President Harrison simply has more on the ball."

"How loyal of you to say so," Judith said. "However, my information indicates that Gregoria has been rigorously neutral throughout its entire history, a preference aided by its smallness, its lack of natural resources, and its apparent ability to juggle the great powers of any particular era to its own benefit. Why should that change now?"

Gavin hesitated. She had done her research, and that he had to admire. But she was getting dangerously close to the truth, and that he could not permit. "Times change, Judith, as do the interests of nations both great and small. Gregoria is anxious to move into the modern world. To do that, it must come to terms with political realities."

"Meaning it must align itself with either us or the U.S.S.R.?"

"Let's just say that it helps to have friends."

"Does King Gregory see it that way?"

"I don't speak for the king," he said.

"I'm looking forward to interviewing him."

"I'm sure he's planning to meet with the media at some point," Gavin said, "to discuss the wedding."

"Which I have no interest in."

"Pity. It will be quite an event."

"Could it be," she ventured, "that it will also conveniently distract attention from something more significant?"

Gavin unfolded his legs. He had finished his brandy and now carefully set the snifter on a nearby table. When he turned back to Judith, his expression was carefully neutral. "You are free, of course, to pursue any idea you think worthwhile. But I'm sure that you're also interested in getting results, and that line of inquiry is a dead end."

"I don't think so."

He watched her mouth as she spoke. In the shadows cast by the single lamp and the fire, her lips looked full and moist. He could almost feel them beneath his own, pliant and yielding.

He stood up and walked over to the mantel, staring down into the flames. His back was to her, but she could sense the tension in the set of his shoulders and the rigid line of his spine. "You're a very stubborn woman."

A tiny shiver of anticipation ran through her. She understood consciously what before she had only allowed herself to sense, that she was deliberately challenging him, knowing what the results would be.

When she didn't reply, he turned around. Their eyes locked as he crossed the room to stand before her. He held out both his hands, the palms raised. Instinctively she put her own in his and allowed herself to be drawn up. The first touch of his hard body against hers made her draw back slightly, only to find that he would not permit it.

"Let's stop sparring with each other, Judith," he murmured. "I can't pretend that I understand what's going on here, but at least I'm willing to admit that we can't ignore it. Will you do the same?"

"I don't..."

His arms tightened around her, compelling truth. "Yes," she whispered, "but it isn't right. I have a job to do. I never bargained on this."

"Neither did I," he said as he bent his head to her. "You're the last thing I expected, lady, and you've turned up at a hell of an inconvenient moment. But that doesn't seem to make any difference."

"We're adults," she protested half-heartedly. "We should be able to control ourselves—"

"Be quiet, Judith."

She should say something, object to his high-handedness, find some way out of the situation. But she couldn't seem to think of anything except the warmth and power of his body, the implacable gentleness with which he held her, and the touch of his mouth on her own.

"Gavin..."

"Shhh. It's all right. You'll see."

And she did, at least there, at that moment, when all rational thought fled and there was only the feel of him claiming her and being claimed. His mouth was gentle yet demanding. The stroke of his tongue as he parted her lips consumed her. Restraint dissolved as though it had never been. She arched against him, a low moan rippling from deep within.

Gavin had not expected to kiss her, had given in to the need reluctantly, and now was stunned by his own response. The more he tasted her, the more he wanted to taste. Her mouth was a silken cavern he could delve in forever. But other delights beckoned: the smooth line of her brow, the shell-like softness of her ear, the sweet curve of her jaw. Each drew his mouth like a moth to fire; each tempted him to linger.

Dimly he was aware of her hands stroking his back through his dinner jacket, of her breasts pressed against his chest and her hips clinging to his. With her in heels, they were almost the same height, their bodies perfectly meshed. He knew she must be aware of his arousal pressing into her, made all the more acute when she did not attempt to pull back.

Judith was beyond any such action. The most basic instincts of self-preservation were falling away from her. She could think only of the man and the remarkable sensations he evoked. When his hands cupped her breasts, the thumbs rubbing lightly over her aching nipples through the thin fabric of her gown and bra, she had to bite down on her lower lip to keep from crying out.

He saw what she did and winced, instantly soothing the small hurt with the stroke of his tongue. His fingers tangled in her thick golden hair, relishing the silken texture as he gently urged her head back. Slowly, meticulously, he placed kisses on her brow, the curve of her cheeks, the delicate line of her nose, coming only at last to her mouth, which parted beneath his like the petals of a flower reaching for the sun.

Judith's hands had slipped beneath his open jacket to stroke the hard planes of his chest. For a moment that was enough, but very quickly she wanted more. Pearl buttons yielded quickly to her agile fingers. His skin was warm, hot even, and dusted with crisp hair that felt rough against her own smoothness. She lowered her head and, without pausing to think about what she was doing, pressed her lips to his bare skin.

A lightning bolt of pleasure shot through Gavin. He stiffened and for the merest instant his hands gripped her almost painfully. "Sweet Judith..."

Dazed by the scent and taste of him, she looked up slowly, meeting the fire in his gaze. Thickly, as though she had all but lost the ability to speak, she whispered, "What's happening to us?"

He laughed harshly, in mockery of the fate that held them helpless. "We're driving each other crazy, and I, for one, can't stand much more."

Three small buttons held the high neck of her dress closed. He got two undone, fumbled with the third and ripped it away. The top of her gown fell forward, leaving only the gold locket gleaming at her throat. He bent his dark head and touched her, first only with the warmth of his breath, then with the moist fire of his lips.

A soft, keening cry broke from Judith. Far in the back of her mind a voice warned that she was losing control of the situation, but she paid scant attention. All the years of rigorous self-discipline were catching up with her. Needs long repressed would no longer be denied. Almost frantically, she curled her fingers in his hair and drew him even closer.

A steely arm wrapped around her waist, holding her immobile. She was bent to the shape of his hard body, to the direction of his will. His mouth, urgently seeking, pushed the fabric further down, revealing the rosy crests of her breasts. At the touch of his tongue against her, Judith quivered. He suckled her with fierce tenderness as his hands played over her, slipping down past her narrow waist to take hold of her hips and press her against him.

The powerful fullness of his manhood made her gasp. Though she was hardly an innocent virgin startled by the physical differences between male and female, she had never before quite perceived what those differences meant. She was made to receive him, to take into her body the driving force of his. An intrinsically primitive need stirred within her. Gone were thoughts of independence, equality, control. All that remained was the savage thirst to know him in the most complete way possible.

Gavin was driven by the same implacable hunger. Without pausing to think, he lowered her onto the couch and came down hard on top of her. Their bodies twisted together, urgent, demanding, almost savage in their wildness. It burned away inhibitions, dissolved caution, melted any thought of control.

Judith's head fell back against the pillows. She clung to him with all the fierce intensity of a woman who has too long denied her own most basic needs.

Not simply for sex, but far more important for affection, for tenderness, for love. Willingly she submerged herself in the touch, taste, and smell of him.

His skin was slightly rough beneath her touch. Rough and hot. His shirt hung open now, bare to the touch of her breasts rubbing against him. She moaned as his mouth moved along her throat and shoulders, trailing fire. His breathing was sharp and ragged, as was her own. When his hands slid beneath the hem of her dress to stroke her thighs, she trembled in anticipation. He stopped briefly when he discovered that she wore not panty hose but a garter belt. A low, sensual chuckle broke from him.

"How I would love," he murmured, "to ask you to stand up and undress for me. But another time. I can't wait."

Neither could she. Even as part of her remained thoroughly shocked by her uncharacteristic behavior, she longed for the culmination of their passion. Later she might very well regret the consequences, but just then she could think of nothing except the hunger he set to raging within her.

Until Gavin abruptly moved away and at the same moment reached for his jacket and threw it over her.

"Daddy..."

The small voice coming from the doorway was so soft as to be all but inaudible. Only a parent long tuned to respond to the slightest need would have heard it.

Gavin had, and just in time. A little boy of about five stood just within the room, clutching a bedraggled teddy bear and looking at the pair on the couch warily.

"Davey," Gavin said, rising swiftly. "What's the matter?"

"I don't feel good." As he spoke, the child's eyes were on Judith. He made no secret of his bewilderment. "Who are you?"

Judith was at an utter loss for words. She had never been in a situation remotely like this one and had no idea of how to respond. Fortunately, Gavin was more adept. Soothingly, he said, "This is a friend of mine, Judith Fairchild." As he spoke, he quickly buttoned his shirt and shoved it back into his trousers. Then he went to his child and put his arms around him.

"Is Nanny asleep?"

The little boy nodded. "Yes, and my stomach hurts." He looked again at Judith. "Maybe I should have waked up Nanny."

"That's all right," his father assured him. "We'll get you back into bed and I'll call Dr. Hamilton. He'll give you something to make you feel better."

Davey nodded trustingly. "I'm sorry to bother you, Daddy."

Judith caught a quick glimpse of Gavin's taut features before he embraced his son tenderly. "You must never say that. You know that I'm always here for you and Jessie."

Davey nodded but continued to stare at Judith. The situation clearly puzzled him, so much that he couldn't even put his bewilderment into words. That told Judith a great deal about Gavin's relationship with his children. He obviously put them above any personal life of his own.

Far from resenting that or being at all put out by the turn of events, she could only admire him all the more for his devotion to his family. That was rare enough in these days, when so many people seemed to feel that only their own feelings and needs mattered. Among extremely powerful, attractive men who could so easily become accustomed to taking without ever giving, it had to be rarer still.

She had hastily restored her clothes and smoothed her hair before she crossed the room to bend down near the child and smile at him reassuringly. "I'm sure you'll be better soon, Davey. But in the meantime, I'm going to leave so your daddy can take care of you."

Gavin shot her a quick glance. He stood up, laid a hand on his son's shoulder and said, "You sit down for a minute. I'm just going to arrange a car for Judith."

As they stepped out into the corridor, he smiled ruefully. "You're being very good about this. Thank you."

"I really do understand," she assured him. "Children have to come first, especially when they aren't feeling well."

Again he gave her the penetrating look that seemed to see right through her. "Not many women would be so tolerant."

"I wouldn't know about that. At any rate . . ." She broke off for an instant, then went on more firmly. "I think it's just as well that Davey interrupted us."

His dark brows drew together. "Regrets, already?"

"Yes, though not as many as I would have had if we'd gone any further."

"You're very frank."

"I have to be in my profession."

They were at the door. A Marine guard snapped to attention when he saw them. Gavin gave quiet orders for a car to be brought around for her. When the guard turned away to see to it, he murmured, "You seem determined that your work will come between us. But given what just happened—and what almost happened—do you think that's realistic?"

Judith suppressed the urge to admit that she was anything but and instead said, "I have to be. There simply isn't any other option."

The smile he gave her was very male, and very knowing. "In my experience, there is nothing more dangerous than deciding on a course that can't possibly be held to."

A long black limousine pulled up in front of them. The driver jumped out and opened the passenger door. Judith lifted the hem of her gown and stepped down the stairs. "That remains to be seen," she said over her shoulder.

Gavin stayed where he was, watching her from the top of the stairs. He stood with his feet planted apart, hands in his pockets, his jacket pushed back to reveal the broad expanse of his chest that she had so recently caressed and reveled in. His hair was tousled, and his eyes gleamed with purely male appreciation.

"You're quite right," he said so softly. "A great deal remains to be seen." Then he laughed, gently but with unmistakable relish.

Judith got into the car and stared straight ahead, resisting the urge to look at him again, knowing that if she did, the temptation to do far more would prove too great to resist.

Chapter 6

In the cold light of day, Judith forced herself to re-member how close she had come the previous night to violating her most basic code of ethics. If Davey hadn't interrupted them when he did, she and Gavin would have shared an experience that would have ir-retrievably hindered her ability to cover the story in Gregoria.

That there was a story she no longer doubted. What she couldn't yet be sure of was exactly how far he was willing to go to prevent her from unearthing it. Not that she wanted to believe that he had deliberately set out to seduce her as a diversion; the mere thought made her stomach twist and caused her to push away her breakfast tray. But like it or not, she had to con-sider the possibility.

A great deal was at stake. If she was right and Gregoria was the site of a deposit of xanium, the ancient kingdom lay at the very hub of a terrifyingly modern conflict. People from either side would go to any lengths to secure the isotope for themselves, because with it would come incalculable power—the power to remain safe behind an impenetrable shield while releasing havoc with impunity.

Surely that wasn't what President Harrison intended. Skeptical she might be, but she couldn't bring herself to believe that there was really any such hideously grandiose conspiracy in the works. It was simply yet another case of powerful men deciding to keep the public in the dark, on the theory that ordinary people couldn't be trusted to respond wisely. And it was exactly that kind of cover-up that the media were responsible for preventing.

So she would do her job, even though that meant keeping Gavin at a distance. Easier said than done, she thought wryly as she stepped out of the shower and wiped the mist from the bathroom mirror. She would have to be in contact with him as she pursued the story, and they were sure to also be thrown together in the course of the royal wedding.

Speaking of which, she really had to do something about an interview with King Gregory. A *private* interview, since she had no intention of tipping her hand in front of her colleagues. She smiled into the mirror as she hastily put on her makeup and brushed her hair. Share and share alike was fine for the playground, but not for the high-pressure environment of television.

No, she would let them find out what she had learned at the same time as everyone else: when she was on the air, breaking the story to the world.

When the phone rang, she was zipping up a pair of pleated beige linen trousers that she had paired with a blue silk blouse. She reached for the receiver with one hand as she lifted her favorite gold chain from the bedside table.

"How the hell do we get out of the airport?" an irate voice demanded without preamble.

Judith grinned. "Hi, Dave, fog clear in Paris?"

"Yeah, unfortunately. I don't believe this place. There's not a cab in sight, nothing but some old guy with—get this—a horse and cart."

"That's Sebastian, and he'll give you a lift if you ask him nicely."

The head of her film crew was silent for a moment, then broke into a resigned laugh. "Trust you to have already figured out how things work around here."

"Not quite," Judith admitted, "but I'm beginning to get an idea. We'll talk about it after you've checked in."

"Fair enough. Is the hotel decent, at least?"

Judith looked around at her room, in which a fairy-tale princess would have felt at home. She thought of Dave—a burly bear of a man—in such a setting and her smile widened. "Uh...it's unusual, but I think you'll get a kick out of it."

"Kicks I can live without," he groused. "Just so long as they got old scotch and strong coffee."

"In that order?"

"You bet. Paris was rough."

"Poor baby. Well, put all that behind you. We've got work to do."

"I get the message," Dave said. "We'll be there as fast as that mangy horse can drag us."

After warning him not to make any such aspersions against Esmerelda in Sebastian's presence, Judith hung up and finished dressing. She figured it would take Dave and the others about an hour to reach the hotel and get reasonably settled. The bar would be open about then, so she'd know where to find them. In the meantime, she intended to do some scouting on her own.

At the royal palace, a press room had been set up, with some apparent reluctance, to handle the tidal wave of inquiries from the international media. Judith had only to show her UBC identification card to be admitted to it. As was usual in such places, tables had been set up with coffee, pastries, and handouts. The last had the least interest for her, but she went through the motions of picking one up and looking it over.

She had barely finished reading it when a petulant voice behind her announced, "If the idea is to be as uninformative as possible, they've succeeded fabulously."

Judith turned to see the familiar face of Danielle Johnson, hostess of the top-rated morning news show and the woman most commonly spoken of as the only true rival to Barbara Walters. Danielle was about forty-five, with meticulously coiffed amber hair, a perfectly made up face, and a figure many women would have killed for. Not too long ago she had done a guest shot on "Dynasty" where she had given Alexis a run for her money, at least in the wardrobe department. Just then she was wearing a perfect little red suit that complemented the fiery snap in her green eyes.

"Hi, Danielle," Judith said pleasantly. "You look terrific."

Her colleague's annoyance faded slightly. She didn't encounter too many other women in the business who were willing to acknowledge her assets. Rivalries were fierce, especially in the field of celebrity interviewing where she had made her mark. But then, Judith Fairchild didn't exactly work in the same field.

Danielle pushed aside the impulse to envy that she felt and smiled. "Good to see you, Judith. What a nice outfit." Actually it was, in the understated way that only leggy blondes with perfect features could get away with.

"Thanks," Judith said. Holding the press release between two fingers, she asked, "So what do you think of this?"

Danielle snorted, a sound reminiscent of her Brooklyn school days when she was chubby little Danielle Jankovich. "It's not worth the paper they printed it on. Honestly, did you ever see such drivel?" Referring to her own copy, she read off, "His Royal Highness was educated at Eton, Georgetown University, and the London School of Economics. He is active in international trade and is a strong proponent of tariff-free markets.'' She gave an exaggerated yawn and delicately covered her mouth with one gloved hand. ''That's not what people want to know, for heaven's sake! Where's the drama, the meat, the sex?''

''Under wraps, from the looks of it,'' Judith said. She had to sympathize with Danielle, whose devoted audience would have found such talk both incomprehensible and excruciatingly boring. Come to think of it, her own audience wouldn't be much more thrilled.

''It's just a wedding,'' she said with a shrug. ''How interesting can it be?''

Danielle looked at her as though she had suddenly grown a second head. ''You're kidding, aren't you? This is the event of the decade. What the world's been waiting for.''

''Oh, come on. The world's waiting for peace, an end to poverty, harmony among nations. Who really cares about two people getting hitched?''

''Yes, well, that's certainly an interesting viewpoint. Is that how you plan to cover it? 'Here we are folks, at just another wedding.' That sort of thing?''

Judith couldn't help but laugh. ''Wouldn't I love to, but the network would have a fit. No, I'll manage to work up some show of enthusiasm. Either that,'' she added, ''or I'll just find something else to talk about.''

No sooner were the words out than she regretted them. This was no time to tip her hand. Fortunately, Danielle didn't seem to pick up on it. She slipped an arm through Judith's and said confidingly, ''A juicy scandal would be nice. Frankly, after Charles and Di, I've had about all the goody-goody I can take."

"Think there's any chance?" Judith asked.

Danielle detached her arm, poured herself a cup of tea, squirted a few drops of fresh lemon into it, and took a sip before she said, "Where there's smoke there's fire. Gregory has sown wild oats all over Europe, the States, and who knows where else. At one time he had no less than three active mistresses, that I was able to find out about. Who knows what else he was up to? Then, with no warning, he announces he's marrying some nobody right out of the schoolroom. Does anyone really believe he's serious about settling down?"

"I suppose not," Judith admitted. Deep inside, in a part of her she normally kept well hidden, she was an incurable romantic who really did believe in the happily ever after. But she also knew that rarely happened in real life. Still, if Danielle was right and the royal marriage was merely a cynical solution on the part of a spoiled monarch intended to give him heirs while leaving him free to amuse himself, he deserved for everyone to know about it.

"Has anyone actually been able to interview Lady Althea?" she asked, figuring that if anyone had the inside track on that, it would be Danielle.

"No, and I don't mind telling you it's beginning to look mighty peculiar." The chagrin she felt after several days of fruitless attempts to meet the bride showed plainly on her carefully maintained features. "The

official word is that she's too busy to meet with reporters. Can you believe that!''

"I'm sure you'll get through to her eventually," she
assured Danielle, although she was really by no means
certain. "She'll tell you all about how she and the king
met, how he proposed, how many bridesmaids she's
going to have, and how many children she plans. Your
viewers will love it."

"Like hell they will. Better she should tell me what
he's like in bed. Not," Danielle added with a worldly
smile, "that it's much of a secret."

"Spare me some of my illusions," Judith said.
"Despite what I do for a living, I still like to think
there's such a thing as privacy."

"Only for ordinary people, my dear. Not for the
rich and famous."

The two women parted a short time later. Danielle
went in search of the hapless information minister
while Judith took advantage of the preoccupation of
her colleagues in the press room, who were making
serious inroads on the trays of pastries, to slip out a
side door into the gardens.

Whatever else might be going on in Gregoria, she
couldn't fault the weather. The day was pleasantly
warm and clear. There was the scent of roses on the air
and the gentle trilling of birds in the nearby trees. She
glanced around to make sure she was unobserved, then
wandered down a gravel path that wound past a fountain in which goldfish swam lazily.

Judith sat down on the stone rim of the fountain,
dipped her hand into the water and let the droplets run

through her fingers. She was feeling very peaceful, which surprised her considering all the unresolved questions clamoring in her mind. But the setting was such that it demanded relaxation, and she was glad enough to give in to it, if only briefly. . . .

Until she saw the girl coming down the path, humming softly to herself and kicking a stone with the tip of a scuffed boot. She walked with her hands thrust into the pockets of her jodphurs. Her body was slender and athletic, her dark hair pulled back into a ponytail that was working itself loose. She had to come closer before Judith could see her features; when she did they were revealed to be lovely with a touch of piquant humor that made them distinctive.

The girl seemed lost in her own thoughts. She had all but reached the fountain when she at last noticed Judith and drew up short. "Why, hello," she said, her voice soft and pleasant. "Where did you spring from?"

"Back there," Judith said, tilting her head toward the palace visible over the tops of the trees. "I suspect I'm trespassing."

"Are you really?" the girl said with a delighted smile. "Well, good. I could do with some company."

A suspicion formed in Judith's mind. She kept her face carefully neutral as she said, "It gets lonely around here?"

"Not exactly." The girl perched on the edge of the fountain and stretched her long legs out in front of her. "There's always people around; in fact, I usually go for a ride in the morning to get some time to myself. But everyone's so busy. It's hard just to get a few minutes to chat.''

''I guess the wedding has everyone on the run.''

The girl rolled her light brown eyes and laughed. ''Does it ever. One would think every single detail was a national crisis. Heavens, people get married all the time.''

Judith couldn't help but raise her eyebrows in surprise. ''But this is a royal wedding, and supposedly the social event of the decade.''

''I guess,'' the girl said reluctantly. ''Still, it's only one day and then...'' Her eyes brightened at the prospect of what came after. ''We'll be able to get back to normal.''

''We'll...''

''Oh, I'm sorry.'' She held out a slender hand with neatly manicured nails. ''I'm Althea.''

''Judith Fairchild, Your Highness.''

Althea made a face. ''Please, not yet. Right now I'm still a plain lady.''

''And I'm a reporter. I think I'd better tell you that right off the bat.''

''Oh, I recognized you,'' Althea said. ''Whenever I'm in the States, I watch you on television. You're very good.''

''Thank you,'' Judith said, hoping she didn't sound as flustered as she felt. Althea had known who she was; furthermore, she apparently traveled frequently. Far from being a sequestered child-fiancée, she was a self-confident, matter-of-fact young woman who clearly knew her own mind.

"Have you been in the States recently?" she asked, as much to gain some time to sort out her own thoughts as because she wanted to know.

"A few months ago. Before the engagement was announced. Since then it's been a little hard to get around."

"Yes...I suppose there are security considerations."

Althea sighed and scuffed her toes in the dirt. "Too many, I sometimes think. At any rate, once we're settled, I'm sure things will get better."

She spoke so confidently that Judith felt compelled to ask, "Have you known King Gregory long?"

Althea gave her a very womanly smile. "All my life."

Which, according to the press release Judith had seen, was twenty years. Not really all that long, though in some ways Althea seemed older than her age.

Perhaps because of the circumstances, comparisons to Princess Diana were inevitable. Judith had seen an interview with the Princess of Wales in which she was very impressed by her sense of knowing exactly what she wanted out of life and how to get it. That was unusual in people of any age, but especially so in young women of sheltered backgrounds. Yet Althea seemed to possess the same trait.

"So now you're getting married. How nice."

Again the womanly smile. "Hmmm, yes. Are you? Married, I mean."

"No, I never have been."

"I didn't think I would be either, at least not for ages."

That was interesting. "Really? Then how did you feel when His Highness proposed?"

"Is this on the record?"

"Not if you don't want it to be."

"I don't, but between you and me, I was tremendously relieved."

"How so?"

"I hadn't thought he'd get around to it for ages yet. He had this idea, you see, that I was too young."

"But he proposed anyway."

"Hmmm, yes. He decided I wasn't, after all." Smile.

Judith was beginning to wonder if Danielle's ideas about this royal love affair were correct in any way at all. She, for one, was beginning to have a touch of sympathy for Gregory, who she suspected had been neatly outmaneuvered. All in his own best interest, of course.

With a sigh, Althea looked at her watch and rose. "I have to get back. There's another fitting due on *The Dress*." She laughed. "Such a fuss over that. State secrets aren't better protected."

"It's fun, though, isn't it, in a way?"

"Oh, sure. But I'm still glad I'll only be going through it once."

Together they walked back along the path. As they turned a corner and the palace came into view, they could see several men standing in the gardens in urgent conversation. One of them was Gavin, his tall,

powerful figure unmistakable to Judith. Beside him
was King Gregory.

Both turned as the women appeared, and for an instant they simply stared at them. "Where," Gregory
demanded, "have you been?"

Althea flushed slightly but did not look surprised.
"I went for a ride."

"So the stable hand reported. You returned a good
forty-five minutes ago. It takes ten minutes to get back
here."

"I walked slowly, and paused to chat." She turned
slightly. "This is Judith Fairchild. She's a reporter on
American television."

The look Gregory gave her suggested that there were
a good many other things he would rather have confronted just then. "How nice. If you'll excuse us, Miss
Fairchild..."

"Wait a moment," Gavin interjected. "Forgive me,
Lady Althea, but did you happen to tell Miss Fairchild anything?"

Both women looked at him frostily. "We chatted,"
Althea said, "off the record." More forcefully, she
added, "There was no harm done."

"Provided that Miss Fairchild intends to respect
your confidence."

Anger rose in Judith. How dare he suggest that she
would do otherwise. "I assure you," she said stiffly,
"that I have no intention of using anything her lady-
ship said." On impulse, she added, "Besides, fascinating though I'm sure the wedding will be, that's not
really what I'm here to cover."

The two men and Althea exchanged a quick glance. Gavin started to speak, but Gregory forestalled him. "Really, Miss Fairchild? Then what is your reason for coming to Gregoria?"

"You might say that there are certain puzzling aspects about current developments here, Your Highness, and that I intend to understand them."

"Very ambitious, considering that you will only be in the country for a few days."

"I have found," Judith said, "that a great deal can be accomplished in very little time provided one is sufficiently determined."

"And you are, Miss Fairchild?"

"I can vouch for that," Gavin muttered. "She's as stubborn as they come."

A flash of humor showed in the king's expression. He held out a hand to Althea, who took it readily. Standing together, the two were a golden couple, both tall and slender, with aristocratic carriages. But there was also something else about them that spoke volumes to Judith and Gavin both: Althea and Gregory were lovers in the truest sense of the word. It showed in the simple affinity of their bodies as they moved together and in the flash of tender passion that lit their eyes when they looked at each other.

"Well, well," Judith said when she was alone with Gavin. Gregory and Althea had excused themselves and gone off with their heads bent close together. The last thing she had heard from them was the soft trill of Althea's laughter in response to something Gregory said. "She certainly isn't what I expected."

"What was that?" Gavin asked. They were following the gravel path toward the main gate. As they walked, he cast her a surreptitious glance. During the night, as he had lain awake staring up at the ceiling and trying to ignore the hunger of his body, he had wondered if she could possibly be as beautiful as he remembered. Now he knew that she was and that the fascination he had felt from the first moment was not only real but even more potent and dangerous than he had realized.

She was moving fast, in the direction he had most feared. By getting close to Althea, she threatened to unravel the whole secret. That he could not allow.

"I thought she would be shy," Judith said. "Not at all self-confident. Someone content to be led around by the nose."

He laughed. "That's as far off the mark as you could get."

"So I've discovered. But tell me—" she turned to look at him "—why is she being kept under wraps?"

"What makes you think she is?"

"Her total unavailability to the media."

"She spoke to you, didn't she?"

"Off the record, and I got the impression it was only because she really needed to talk to someone."

"You're imagining things," Gavin said. "Lady Althea is extremely busy with preparations for the wedding."

"I also got the impression she was leaving most of that to others, and in fact was anxious for it to be over."

Rather than try to respond directly, he took a chance and pretended to brush off her concern. "What do you care, anyway? You said yourself that the wedding doesn't interest you."

"True, but Lady Althea does. There's something about her situation...."

"Let it go, Judith." He had stopped walking, and automatically she had done the same. They faced each other on the path, scant inches apart. His eyes were intent, his mouth hard and determined. "I've tried to tell you before, but now I'm going to spell it out. You're walking straight into trouble of the worst sort. Even if there wasn't any... personal element between us, I couldn't stand by and watch you do that."

Judith flushed. She felt the heat stain her cheeks and despised herself for it, but the reaction couldn't be suppressed. Ever since she'd seen him standing beside the king, so tall and strong in the morning sunlight, she had been fighting memories of the previous night. Her body still resonated to the power of his touch and her heart still ached for what might have been.

Both of which she resented. "Let's get something straight. You're no more responsible for me than I am for you. We both have jobs to do, which may very well place us on opposite sides. The best thing we can do is to stay out of each other's way."

Gavin's mouth tightened further and he had to keep a firm rein on his temper. Part of him wanted her to acknowledge that he was right and willingly depend on him for guidance and protection. That she would not irked him even as it increased his admiration for her.

"That's hardly possible," he said. "If you carry out your intention of pursuing a story other than the wedding—" he was picking his words very carefully "—you will get in my way and I will have to stop you."

"Is that a threat?"

"Take it however you like."

"You realize that threatening a news person is a bad idea? It only makes us all the more determined. Besides—" she looked at him directly "—you've just told me that there definitely is a story and that I'm getting closer."

He took a deep breath, willing himself to patience. They started walking again, still side by side, but the distance between them was greater than before. Each was mindful of the dangers involved in getting too close.

"Look," he said finally, "suppose we make a deal. I'll tell you what I can, off the record, and when the time comes to break the story, you'll have first crack at it."

Judith thought that over carefully. She had accepted such arrangements in the past when she believed they were merited. Generally speaking, they had worked out well. "All right, I'm willing to give it a try. But I'll expect your full cooperation."

"That isn't what I offered," he hedged. "There are limits to what you can be told. However, I'll assure you that what you do find out will be enough for an exclusive that will rock the country, if not the world."

She could hardly claim to be satisfied with less. And she had to admit that he had gone far out on a limb by telling her so much already. She was more convinced than ever that xanium lay at the heart of the story; nothing else could be of such consequence.

"You have a deal," she said quietly.

"Not so fast. There's one other thing you should know about before you agree."

"The proverbial catch?"

"If you like. I won't brief you here in the capital. You'll have to agree to stay at a place I designate until the story can be told."

"That's crazy! I'm supposed to be covering the wedding."

"You'll have to work that out with New York," he insisted.

Judith thought over what he was asking, or, more correctly, demanding. It hurt to know that he didn't trust her, but she had to admit that under the circumstances she couldn't blame him. Too much was at stake to risk any leak of the story. "How long would I have to be ... incommunicado?"

"I don't know exactly," he said. "A week perhaps, not much more than that."

"And at the end, I'd have the story exclusively?"

"That's my offer."

"You're asking a lot," she said frankly. "For all I know, you'll squirrel me away somewhere and I'll never hear a word about what's going on."

"Yes, I could do that," he admitted, his tone making it clear that he had considered it. Overhead, the sun burst through the canopy of trees that stretched beside the path. He stopped and smiled at her. "On the other hand, you could decide to trust me."

That was very hard for Judith. Her profession did not incline her to give trust easily. But more than that, the effect he had on her—the personal element, as he had said—was a warning flag she thought she would be wise to heed.

Unfortunately, she couldn't. Not when it might mean missing a once-in-a-lifetime story.

"All right," she said finally. "I'll call New York and see what I can work out."

"Good. You can let me know the results tonight."

"Tonight?"

"I'm giving a small dinner party. I'd like you to attend."

"That's very nice of you, but I have a great deal to—"

"King Gregory will be there. It would be a good idea for him to get to know you before you're brought into the picture."

Judith could hardly fault the logic of that, any more than she could deny that she badly wanted to be with Gavin again. Reluctantly, feeling not unlike the way she had the first time she walked out on a high diving board, she agreed.

Chapter 7

The dinner party turned out to be more enjoyable than Judith had expected. King Gregory and Lady Althea were the only guests, the setting was relaxed and informal, and the conversation proved lively, though anything to do with business—whatever that might be—was carefully ignored.

They talked about Gregoria—its history, culture, and the haphazard way in which it had all come into being in the first place. "My illustrious ancestor," Gregory said, "King Gregory the First was seventeen when he left England on the Crusade. He was a younger son with no prospects at home who apparently dreamed of making his fortune in the Holy Land."

"You make him sound like some well-scrubbed youth out of—what was that American writer's name—Horatio Alger?" Althea teased.

"Far from it," Gregory acknowledged. "Like just about everyone else back then, he was as bloodthirsty as they came. After slashing and maiming his way through half a dozen battles, he'd acquired enough booty to plan on returning home, buying himself a nice estate and settling down to raise a gaggle of little Gregorys."

"What happened?" Judith asked. She was seated next to Gregory in the small dining room. Gavin was facing her. He looked more at ease than she had seen him before, though his gaze continued to be wary whenever their eyes met.

"He got lost," Althea said. "Instead of reaching southern Spain, where he could have gotten a ship for home, he landed here."

"He had with him two dozen foot soldiers who had served with him in the Holy Land," the king explained. "They found a local peasantry being bled to death by a rapacious warlord. Gregory was deeply offended by what he saw and determined to right it, not to mention that he also knew a good opportunity when he stumbled over it."

"He tidied things up in record time," Gavin interjected. "It was a classic case of superior strategy and weaponry crushing an opponent who barely knew what hit him."

His Highness inclined his head slightly in acknowledgment of the compliment. "Gregory sent home for a bride and settled down to rule. He lived another forty years and had one son and seven daughters. The former inherited the crown, while the latter made advantageous political marriages with the surrounding principalities. By the time Gregory was laid to rest, his dynasty was on solid ground.''

''Where it has remained,'' Judith mused, ''to this time.''

''And where it will remain,'' Gregory said firmly, ''well into the next century and beyond.''

She was inclined to believe him. Almost every other monarchy had long since faded away, and those that remained were mere figureheads, except for the royal house of Gregory, which continued to wield considerable power. And stood poised to wield even more.

Understanding the implicit ground rules of the dinner, she could not mention what was uppermost on her mind, a restriction that chafed but that she managed to tolerate with good grace. It was a decided improvement, after all, over her conversation with Sam Wexman.

Sam had been incredulous at first when she told him what she was prepared to agree to in order to get what she believed would be a major story. ''You're actually going to let yourself be locked away somewhere,'' he had demanded, ''strictly on Penderast's word that he'll make it worth your while?''

''I don't see what choice I have,'' she countered, holding on to the phone as tightly as she clung to her patience. ''If I reject his terms, he'll do everything he can to stop me from getting to the bottom of what's going on here. It's possible he could even get me kicked out of the country. On the other hand, if I go along with him, he promises to tell me everything he can."

"That's no promise at all. You'll be lucky to get the time of day from him."

"I realize there's risk involved...."

"Risk I can live with," he shot back. "This is something different. Do it his way and you'll be completely dependent on him. You won't be able to pursue other leads or sources. He'll call the tune and you'll have to dance to it."

Judith did not like the picture he painted, on any number of levels. Professionally she would be in a very difficult position, but personally she might be even worse off. Still, she couldn't come up with an alternative. Which raised the touchy subject of whether or not she was really trying hard to find another way.

"What do you want me to do, Sam?" she demanded finally. "If I refuse, I've blown the story. I'm convinced of that. Gregoria is simply too small and tightly knit for anyone to be able to snoop around without getting caught. We're on to something really big, but it could go straight through our fingers if we try to get it on our terms."

There was a moment's silence before Sam said gruffly, "This guy has really gotten to you, hasn't he?"

"What guy?"

"Penderast. Who do you think I'm talking about?"

"Well, King Gregory is very attractive...."

"Cut it out, Judith; it won't fly. I know damn well it isn't like you to be snowed, but it can happen to the best of us once."

"Not to me," she said flatly even as she prayed it was true. "Gavin—Ambassador Penderast—and I are simply trying to work out an arrangement that will protect both our interests."

Sam remained skeptical, but in the end he'd had no choice but to agree, with the stipulation that she stay in close contact with him. "I don't care if it has to go through Penderast, I want to know if you're all right."

"You'll believe him?"

"No, so here's the code we'll use." She listened as he outlined a series of key words that would alert him to the presence or absence of danger. Only then was she at last able to get off the phone and get ready for dinner.

Gregory and Althea stayed until shortly after midnight. Judith was both sorry and relieved to see them go. She had enjoyed their company, but as the evening wore on, her thoughts turned increasingly to what would happen when she was alone with Gavin.

She briefly considered leaving with the royal couple on the excuse that she had a great deal to do the next day, but that was a coward's way out and she wouldn't take it. Instead, she agreed to Gavin's suggestion that they share an after-dinner drink while they discussed what would happen next.

"I think you should plan to leave the capital tomorrow," he said when they were seated in a small parlor that adjoined the dining room. She was grate-

ful that he hadn't suggested the library where she suspected they would both have had difficulty keeping
their minds on the business at hand.

It was hard enough under the circumstances. Already she knew him well enough to tell that he was
tired. The lines around his eyes were more deeply
etched, and his movements were slightly slower than
usual. He had loosened his tie and run a hand through
his thick hair. Those gestures, too, were familiar to her
now. Odd how quickly she was getting to know such
small personal things about him.

Determinedly, she drew her mind back to other
matters. "I don't intend going anywhere until I have
a much clearer idea of what it is we're talking about."

He raised an eyebrow. "I thought you already knew
everything there was to, about it."

"Hardly, or I wouldn't need you."

"But you do, don't you?" He leaned closer, observing her intently. "This story means an enormous
amount to you."

"Of course I care about it...." For an instant she
was tempted to add that she also cared about him, but
she suppressed the impulse almost at once. Nothing
could be more foolhardy.

"Enough to take a major risk in order to get it?"

"Because you've given me no choice."

"That's true," he admitted. "I've found that
sometimes it's wiser not to leave any room for maneuvering."

Judith didn't like the sound of that, though she
couldn't say for sure why it bothered her. Granted, it

was unpleasant to think that she had been pushed into a corner where she had no choice but to agree to his terms. Still, such things happened in her business. What she suspected lay at the root of her unease was the growing sense that they weren't talking about business, or at least not strictly. The personal undercurrents between them were far too powerful to ignore.

Still, she wanted the story. And perhaps something more that she wasn't ready to acknowledge. Quietly, she said, "Why don't we put our cards on the table, Gavin? I believe that a deposit of xanium has been found here in Gregoria and that you're negotiating with the king to secure it for the United States. If you will simply admit that's true and agree to fill me in on the details when we get wherever it is we're going, then I'll agree to leave the capital tomorrow." She glanced at her watch and smiled slightly. "Or, more correctly, today."

Gavin looked at her for a long moment. She returned his gaze with what she hoped was the correct blend of understanding and determination. No one had to explain to her the difficulty of his position. He was undoubtedly sworn to protect the security of his mission. To tell her anything at all would violate that, but it was also, as he had recognized, his best chance of keeping the lid on the story until he chose to remove it.

"You're right," he said. "There is xanium here, and we're hoping to get it. Damn it, we have to." He stood up abruptly, his hands thrust into his trouser pockets.

"Somehow I have to make Gregory understand. The stakes are simply too high for him to try to go it alone."

"Is that what he's trying?" Judith asked.

"The closest thing to it. He still believes he can maintain Gregoria's neutrality."

"Can you blame him? It's served them well all these centuries." Indeed it had. She couldn't remember ever being in a place where the people had a stronger sense of their own security. That, more than anything else, would enable them to make the transition to the modern world peacefully. Provided it could last.

"But times change," Gavin insisted. "With xanium here, Gregory has no choice but to align himself with one of the superpowers."

"I can't imagine him siding with the Soviets."

"No, neither can I, but that isn't the point. The longer he delays, the more the Russians will be tempted to intervene. There's already a small underground opposition that with sufficient support could be turned into something much worse."

Judith couldn't bring herself to believe him. Granted, what he was describing had happened in other countries, but in Gregoria? "I don't see how the people here could go for that."

"They wouldn't have to. All it takes to stage a revolution is a sufficiently determined cadre of fanatics with the proper weapons. And I'm not talking only about guns. Terrorism, murder, kidnapping, are the tools of oppression."

"There's been none of that here."

"Yet. But it could be coming, which is why Gregory has to make a decision soon."

The thought of the peaceful kingdom being swept by the brutality that polluted the outside world made Judith feel ill. She could understand Gavin's determination to prevent that, but she could also see why Gregory was reluctant to place his trust in another nation, no matter how worthy of that trust it might be.

Judith had enough faith in her country to believe that it really would do everything it could to help Gregoria. However, she was also enough of a realist to know that might not be enough. Though she wouldn't say so to Gavin, she had to feel that the king was right to be reluctant and to be searching for a better alternative. She only hoped he would find it before it was too late.

"I should be going," she said as she rose.

"Judith, about last night . . ." They were standing close together. She wasn't sure how that had happened. A pulse beat at the base of his throat where he had undone his shirt. She remembered pressing her lips there and flushed.

"I don't want to talk about that."

The corners of his mouth lifted. "Surely it wasn't all that bad."

"It was a mistake."

"So you've made clear. I, however, disagree."

The look she shot him was so stricken that he couldn't help but regret his impetuosity. He might even have said so if she hadn't so swiftly suppressed her concern, replacing it by a cold flash of anger.

"It doesn't really matter whether you do or not," she said. "Our relationship is strictly business."

Wryly he reflected that nothing she could say could challenge him more. Did she realize it, if only subconsciously, or did she really believe the situation had not yet slipped beyond their control?

Whichever the case might be, he saw no profit in arguing with her. Direct disagreement had never been his style. As a diplomat he had long since learned to cope with conflicting views, and often enough to reconcile them in a direction that served his own purposes.

"Let's not worry about it right now," he suggested soothingly. "I'll pick you up tomorrow—say about ten a.m.—and we'll drive out to where you'll be staying."

"Where is that?" Judith asked. She was vividly aware of his hand on her bare arm. His touch was light but familiar, as though he were letting her know that he would not be kept at a distance.

He smiled gently. "I'll tell you tomorrow."

"Don't you think that's carrying things too far?"

"No, but I can see how you might."

Judith suppressed an annoyed sigh. How was she supposed to fight with someone who always managed to sound so reasonable and understanding? As a tactic that was hard to beat: be completely sympathetic to your opponent's view, but never give an inch on your own, until you absolutely had to. As it was, she had no weapons to try to enforce a compromise. Gavin held all the cards. Worse yet, he knew it.

"No wonder you do so well at negotiations," she murmured under her breath.

"What's that?"

"Nothing. I was merely commenting on your propensity for getting your own way."

They stepped out on the portico. The Marine guard spotted them and immediately raised his arm to summon the waiting limousine. Gavin's hand fell away from her arm. He stood silhouetted against the light from the entry, a tall, broad figure who dominated even so impressive a setting.

"I'm glad you realize that," he said softly before he took her hand in his and raised it to his lips. The gesture, usually so foreign to an American male, was made with complete naturalness. As a gracious salute to her beauty and femininity, it could not help but have a pleasing effect on Judith. But she also recognized it as a warning that her hopes of keeping their relationship impersonal were already under concerted attack. Not only from him but also from her own unruly impulses.

Gavin remained on the portico until after the car carrying her had pulled away. His eyes were hooded and his expression inscrutable. Only the rapid beat of the pulse in his throat signaled his arousal, and his determination.

Only reluctantly did he turn away and reenter the embassy. It was late, and he was anxious to check on his children and get to bed. But one more task needed to be done.

In the privacy of the library, he dialed a number he already knew well. The phone at the other end rang twice before Ambassador Leonid Karischenekov answered his private line.

Chapter 8

It was raining when Judith woke up the next morning. She opened one eye and from her safe nest in the bed looked dubiously toward the window. The briefest glance sent her burrowing into the covers, until she remembered what it was she was supposed to do that day.

Leave the capital, go to some unexplained place with Gavin, get the scoop of the century.

A rude expression she would not normally have used found its way past her lips. She must have been batty to agree to his terms. Hadn't he already told her enough for her to break the story? Sure, she wouldn't be able to use his name, because he'd talked off the record, but plenty of correspondents got by referring to "highly placed sources."

Sam would let her do it, too. In fact, he'd probably string her up if he even knew she was waffling. She didn't like to speculate about why she had promised Gavin that she would wait. Part of it was because he had held out the lure of more details, but that was only the tip of the iceberg. She knew that she also had some doubts about breaking a story that might actually harm her country despite the public's right to know— a moral dilemma that tormented all good journalists at one time or another. But beyond all that was the simple fact that she couldn't bear to disappoint Gavin. She suspected that his frankness was a test, which, much as she resented it, she didn't want to fail.

With a grumble of discontent with him, herself, the world in general, she threw back the covers and got out of bed. The air was unexpectedly cool. She shivered as she picked up her robe and hastily pulled it on.

Rainy days always depressed her. The best strategy she had ever devised for dealing with them was to stay in bed with a good book and a pint of ice cream. But often enough she had forgone such pleasures in order to get on with a job.

An hour later, fortified by a pot of coffee and a breakfast that would have done a lumberjack proud, she packed her bag and headed downstairs to the lobby. A few words with the clerk at the reception desk were enough to clarify that she wasn't checking out, merely planning to be away for a few days.

At any rate, she hoped it would be a few. Gavin had said a week, perhaps a little longer. She could stand that, if only just. But if it dragged on . . .

Rather than dwell on that, she occupied herself by browsing through a rack of newspapers and magazines. There was a good international selection in half a dozen languages. She picked out a pile, even throwing in a couple of fashion magazines she generally didn't bother with. There was no telling what the reading material would be like where she was going, so it would be wise to stock up.

She was paying for them when out of the corner of her eye she saw Jim West enter the hotel newsstand, and suppressed a groan. He caught sight of her at the same time and headed straight in her direction.

"Glad I ran into you," he said. "Just heard there's going to be a briefing on the wedding at the palace this morning. We can go over together."

His easy presumption that she would be glad of his company annoyed Judith, but she gave no sign of that. "Thanks, Jim, but I'm going to be busy."

He hunched his shoulders and frowned at her. "I know you're not crazy about this assignment, honey, but if you don't mind a little advice, you ought to take it more seriously. Skipping briefings is bad policy."

The idea of him telling her how to behave brought a dangerous gleam into Judith's eyes, but she merely shrugged. "I'll keep that in mind...sweetheart."

He did a quick double take before it dawned on him that she was chiding his familiarity. West flushed, and his rather full mouth took on a sullen pout. "Suit yourself. I guess you big-deal correspondents figure you don't have to follow the same rules as the rest of us."

No way she was going to rise to that bait. "Whatever you say. Now, if you'll excuse me . . ."

She finished paying for her purchases and went to move past him, only to find that he childishly blocked her way. "I saw you dancing with Penderast the other night."

"So?"

"Get anything good?"

"If I did," she snapped, no longer trying to hide her irritation, "I'd hardly tell you."

"Why not? We could do each other a favor."

"I doubt it."

Resigned to going around him, she started to do so, only to be stopped when he held out a hand. "Wait a minute. I'm not kidding. If we trade info, we'll both be out ahead."

Judith was no stranger to such arrangements between colleagues; she had participated in a few, but only with men and women she truly respected and trusted. West fit neither category.

"Thanks all the same," she said with a pointed look at his hand, "but I prefer to do my own leg work."

He gave her a broad grin that exposed a great many capped teeth. "You'll be shortchanging yourself this time."

His confidence surprised Judith. She thought him perfectly capable of exaggerating, even lying, but suspected that she could pick up on that easily enough. All she was getting from him was complete assurance that he had something of great value to offer.

"Course," he said, "I don't know what you've found out so far. Maybe it's peanuts."

Judith carefully schooled her expression to give no hint of how wrong he was. "Maybe, but I'll take the risk. Now I really have to be going." She had caught sight of Gavin in the lobby, looking around for her.

"What's the rush?" West asked. He turned to glance in the same direction and his eyes narrowed. "Well, well, our illustrious ambassador. Wonder what he's doing here."

Judith brushed past him without answering. She walked into the lobby, caught Gavin's eye and, as he started toward her, gave an all but imperceptible shake of her head. As she had hoped, he understood and stopped where he was, pretending interest in a display of jewels in the window of an exclusive boutique, one of several in the lobby.

Feeling West's eyes boring into her back, she hurried through the main entrance and out into the rain. Unsure of what to do, she began walking in the direction away from the palace. She had gotten about two blocks when a black Porsche pulled up beside her.

"Get in," Gavin said as he leaned over to open the door on the passenger side.

She was glad enough to do as he said, particularly since she had just remembered that her one and only umbrella was safe and dry in her New York apartment. Her hair was soaked, her cotton jacket and slacks stuck to her, and she could feel a sneeze coming on.

As she fumbled in her pocket for a tissue, he turned up the heater and stepped on the accelerator. "What was that about, anyway?"

Judith leaned back against the seat. "I didn't want Jim West to see us together."

"West . . . he's a stringer for another network, isn't he?" When she affirmed that, Gavin asked, "Professional rivalry?"

"Hardly. I get along fine with just about everyone in the business, but there's something about him. . . ."

She didn't elaborate, nor did he press her. They drove in silence through the rain-spattered streets of the capital. Once they were across an ancient stone bridge, the buildings rapidly gave way to rolling fields and meadows green with young shoots of wheat and corn. Judith, who had lived for years in Los Angeles before she'd moved to New York, never failed to be surprised at how close certain cities were to the countryside, as though they were only a minor afterthought of a people whose soul was still firmly entrenched in the fertile soil.

"Did you have any trouble getting away?" Gavin asked at length. He was not a man normally made uneasy by silence, but the quiet intimacy they had slipped into left him unusually wary. He told himself that he would be a fool to get too comfortable with her. It was fine that he wanted to take her to bed, something he fully intended doing in the not very distant future, but anything beyond that would be courting disaster.

Above all, no matter how he longed to, he couldn't trust her. She was a tough, hard-nosed reporter out for a major story. He had to keep reminding himself that was the only reason she had agreed to his terms. Cynicism offered a refuge of sorts. He was feeling more in control when she said, "I had to tell my chief cameraman what was going on."

"Why?" Gavin demanded. He could understand her having to clear it with New York, but to tell someone who was right on the scene in Gregoria...

"Because if I hadn't, he would have asked awkward questions." Actually, Dave had done that anyway. Only his call to Sam Wexman had convinced him that Judith hadn't taken leave of her senses, and had secured his cooperation in covering for her.

"The story," she explained, "is that I've been taken ill and have returned to New York for medical treatment. I presume you can arrange for that to be corroborated here."

He nodded. "I'll make a call when we get where we're going. That will take care of it."

"About our destination, don't you think you could reveal it now?"

He thought that over for a moment before agreeing. There was little enough she could do short of jumping out of the car. "I've borrowed the royal hunting lodge."

Judith absorbed this information in silence before she said, "It pays to have friends."

"His Highness has been most understanding."

"Then he approves of your telling me what's going on?"

"No, but he realizes that we have no choice. Not if we don't want to see the story released before we're ready."

Judith realized that he had indirectly complimented her by acknowledging that she could unearth the story without his cooperation.

"Does that mean," she asked, "that an accord has been reached between the U.S. and Gregoria?"

Gavin suppressed a sigh. They hadn't even reached the lodge yet and already she was interviewing him. "No, it doesn't, but we are making progress and neither one of us wants to see our talks derailed by premature publicity."

For a moment, Judith felt a stab of guilt that she hadn't been willing to simply forgo breaking the story until the negotiations were finished. But she pushed that aside as swiftly as it had arisen. The deal she had made with Gavin gave them both what they wanted; neither side would lose out. Provided they both kept their word.

"The royal hunting lodge sounds very grand," she said in a bid to interrupt the heavy silence that had settled over them. "Are you sure we won't attract undue attention there?"

To her surprise, he flashed her a smile. "I'm sure." When he didn't elaborate, she had to be content with that rather cryptic rejoinder.

The powerful car ate up the miles. As the road beyond the capital narrowed and traffic petered out to

almost nothing, Judith put her head back and dozed.
From time to time she surfaced enough to be aware of
the rain still spattering against the windshield and of
the solid warmth of the man next to her.

In that half state between consciousness and sleep,
her defenses were lowered. She was able to admit, if
only to herself, how glad she was to be with him. He
at once excited her and made her feel safe, which was
either dangerous or absurd, or both. For the ump-
teenth time, she reminded herself that she had a job to
do. Anything she allowed to get in the way of it would
undoubtedly be regretted later.

"We're here," Gavin said softly.

She opened her eyes to find him looking at her with
an expression she could not quite define. It seemed
made up of equal parts tenderness, caution, and determination. There was no time to puzzle over it before he helped her out of the car.

The rain had stopped. A few brave rays of sunshine
were trying to poke out through the scudding clouds.
They touched the rustic pile of logs with slender darts
of gold.

"That's a hunting lodge, all right," Judith murmured. It could hardly be anything else. Rough-hewn
logs stained black by pitch and weather rose to a
peaked roof on which exotic mythical creatures were
stenciled in a riot of reds and oranges. Leaded windows complete with shutters dotted the front and sides
of the building. To complete the image of another era
in which rugged masculinity was untrammeled, there

was an oak door with cross beams that bore what looked like hatchet marks.

"Really great, isn't it?" Gavin said with a grin. He had gotten their bags out of the car. "You'll see imitations all over the States, but this is the real thing."

"If you say so," Judith murmured dubiously. All she could imagine was great burly men tromping back from the hunt to swill beer and sing while bloody carcasses dripped outside. It was hardly her idea of a hideaway paradise.

"Ever been hunting?" Gavin asked cheerfully as he pushed open the door and stood aside for her to enter.

"No, to be frank, the mere idea makes me sick." She was about to step inside, only to be stopped flat by what met her eyes. In sharp contrast to the rough exterior, the room they entered was the epitome of almost barbaric lavishness and sensuality.

Oriental carpets any New York antique dealer would have killed for glowed against the polished wood floor. Overstuffed divans covered with throw pillows faced an intricately carved fireplace. From the ceiling hung diaphanous curtains which continued on down the walls. Copper braziers were lit, dispelling any dampness and adding to the faint light streaming past the veiled windows.

"There are servants here," Gavin explained, "but they're extremely discreet."

"I'm beginning to see why," Judith said dryly. "Exactly what kind of hunting did the Gregorian nobility go in for?"

"The amorous kind, of course. The lodge was built by Gregory's great-grandfather. It's been maintained into the present era as a kind of . . . memorial."

"Mmmm."

"All right, it's been more than that. But Gregory's reformed. I wouldn't be surprised if he and Althea put in a nursery here."

"They'd better do something about this fireplace first," Judith said. She was peering more closely at the intricately carved mantel and, despite herself, blushing. The nude male and female figures, intertwined in explicit poses, banished any doubt she might have had about the type of sport to which the lodge was dedicated. And raised a whole new series of questions.

"Gavin, exactly how did you happen to pick this place?"

"I didn't," he said ingenuously as he started up the stairs to the second floor. "Gregory suggested it."

Following him, she muttered, "How obliging of His Highness."

Gavin stopped on the landing and looked at her with grave innocence. "Judith, surely you aren't suggesting that I had any ulterior motive in bringing you here."

"I hope not, because if you did, you're bound to be disappointed."

She managed to say that with far more conviction than she actually felt, but he looked singularly unperturbed. "If you don't mind," she added briskly, "I'd like to get started on the interview as soon as possible."

"I thought we already had," he muttered under his breath. More audibly, he said, "I'll meet you downstairs in an hour. We'll have lunch and I'll start filling you in."

And what was she supposed to do for an hour? Judith wondered after she had entered her room. It looked like something out of a harem, complete with an immense circular bed and a sunken marble tub that looked as though it could hold a very friendly crowd. Unpacking took all of five minutes, which left her with plenty of time to twiddle her thumbs. She flopped down on the bed for a moment, but the ceiling mural of leering gods and goddesses disporting themselves was too much for her and she got up again hastily.

She was standing in the middle of the room with her fists clenched when the humor of the situation struck her. For the first time in her life, she was in what certainly qualified as a "love nest" and she couldn't even enjoy it. Sam would love the irony of that; someday she might even tell him about it. But in the meantime, she couldn't see any reason not to unbend enough to take advantage of some of the room's special features, chief among them the tub.

When it was filled with steaming water liberally scented by the bottles of exotic oils she found on the rim, she stripped off her clothes and submerged herself in the silken heat. A long sigh, almost a purr, escaped her. Shamefully hedonistic it might be, but she was going to indulge in a nice long soak and possibly even keep Gavin waiting. The man definitely had an autocratic streak, and it was past time he learned that she wouldn't automatically fall in with his plans.

That thought pleased her enough that she stretched out, wiggling her toes, and grinned in the mirror thoughtfully positioned in front of the tub. Why anyone would particularly want to observe herself—or himself...or themselves—bathing was beyond her. She stuck out her tongue at her reflection and reached for a sponge.

Fifteen minutes later, squeaky clean, she gazed up at the shameless ceiling and calculated what a person could do in such a grandiose tub. Sip champagne and nibble on strawberries. Compose erotic poetry. Or...

Or indeed. Time she got out before she turned into a prune. She rose, the water sluicing off her, and reached for a towel. Just as the door opened and Gavin walked in.

Chapter 9

It was an honest mistake. At least he thought it was. In the dim light of the hallway, it had been hard to tell the door to his room from all the others. And preoccupied as he was by the phone call he'd just placed to Gregory, he'd simply walked in and found her....

"I'm sorry," he said automatically, his eyes riveted on the gleaming length of her naked body. "I thought this was my room...."

"Well, it obviously isn't," Judith choked. Belatedly she thought to clutch the towel to her. Not that it gave her much of a feeling of protection. But then a full suit of armor wouldn't have accomplished that. Not when she was confronted by the smoldering look in Gavin's hazel eyes and the abrupt tautness of his body.

"If you wouldn't mind leaving," she said, sounding more shaky than sarcastic.

"Oh, yes...of course." Leave. Turn around and walk out the door. You've embarrassed her enough, not to mention how the mere sight of her is tormenting you.

He turned, his hand on the doorknob. "I'll wait downstairs for you."

"Fine." Still clutching the towel, furiously aware of the tremors racing through her, she went to step out of the sunken tub. Only to have her foot come down on the soap she had left on the rim. *"Ohhh..."* Flailing her arms in a futile effort to regain her balance, she let the towel drop.

Gavin, turning back at her startled exclamation, was treated to yet another glimpse of her beauty. But this time he recovered far faster and managed to cross the room in swift strides, to catch her up in strong arms before she could hit the floor.

"Are you all right?" he asked as he cradled her against his chest, looking down at her bemusedly.

"Ah...yes, thank you."

"You have to be more careful around tubs. Don't you know that something like fifty percent of all accidents happen in bathrooms?"

"This is a bedroom."

"Yes...well, accidents happen there, too."

Judith had the uncanny feeling that she was about to be caught up in one of them. Or was it an accident? With her body pressed against his, the strength of his arms around her and the warmth of his skin seeping through to hers, she had to wonder if this hadn't been ordained from the moment they met, if not before.

She really should say something, suggest that he put her down, remind him that they weren't going to get involved—something. Except that between her mind and her vocal cords, some connection seemed to have snapped. Her heart was beating very rapidly, or was that his? It was getting very hard to tell the difference.

"Gavin . . . ?"

He met her eyes and smiled very tenderly. "It's all right."

"No, it can't be. . . ."

He had crossed the room to the edge of the bed, where he put her down gently. "So stubborn." He made it sound like a caress, as though there was nothing he liked better about her. Well, perhaps a few things. "You have the loveliest skin."

Of which he was seeing a great deal. She made a belated effort to reach for the spread with some distant intention of covering herself, but he would not permit it. His large hand covered hers as he said, "Judith, any good diplomat can tell you when it's time to accept the inevitable."

"Nothing's inevitable. We're in control of our own lives." The note of desperation in her voice appalled her. Was she really so afraid of losing control, or even of relinquishing it briefly?

Tentatively she reached out a hand, touching the broad expanse of his shoulder. It was reassuringly solid, like the man himself. He exuded an air of calmness and stability even in the midst of unmistakable passion.

A long breath escaped her. "Gavin...I haven't done this very recently."

If he was surprised, he didn't show it. Instead, he stroked her cheek gently before his finger came to rest lightly on the fullness of her lower lip. "That's all right. Neither have I."

"You haven't...?"

"Since Carrie died, sex hasn't been a high priority with me. Oh, I've indulged from time to time, but with about the same degree of enthusiasm I bring to a cold shower." He grimaced self-deprecatingly. "I know that hasn't been fair to the women I've known, but I haven't been able to do anything about it. Until now."

Should she believe him? It was tempting to, of course, but Judith thought of herself as a sophisticated woman and nobody's fool. He might simply have stumbled across an extremely effective line.

Her attempt at cynicism failed utterly, partly because it was foreign to her nature but also because her body was beginning to hum with pleasure that quite simply eclipsed all else. And all because he was stroking her, lightly and gently, a hand—the palm surprisingly callused—running down her arm, dipping into the indentation of her waist, coming to rest on the curve of her hip.

"This doesn't seem quite fair," she murmured.

His eyebrows rose. "How's that?"

"You dressed, me not."

"I see what you mean."

He rose from the bed and stepped back, then matter-of-factly began removing his clothes. He watched her as he did so, seeing where her eyes drifted, watching them widen, smiling as they grew heavy-lidded with desire.

"That's very flattering," he said when he was naked, still standing before her.

Her mouth was dry. She licked her lips before responding. "What is?"

"The way you look at a man."

"You're...easy to look at." Actually he wasn't. There was an odd mixture of the compelling and the intimidating about his physique. The broad sweep of his shoulders gave way to a heavily muscled chest. His waist and hips were narrow, his thighs long and powerful. Between them, nestled in dark curls, was his manhood.

A faint smile touched Judith's mouth. She was remembering the days of her adolescence when she and her friends talked in mingled whispers and giggles about what boys had "down there." The first time she had seen a naked man she had caught herself thinking that nature might consider going back to the drawing board for another try.

Looking at Gavin, she changed her mind. He was beautiful in an intrinsically male way that called to everything female in her. Hardly aware that she did so, she held out her arms to him.

He needed no further invitation. With the swiftness of a man too long starved for a necessity of life, he came to her. Tremors coursed through his long, powerful body. She matched them with her own as he wrapped an arm around her waist, drawing her closer. His hand slid lower to savor the satiny smoothness of her buttocks.

"It's funny," she murmured, only realizing after the fact that she had spoken out loud.

"Funny?"

She touched his chest tentatively, liking the strength and solidity she felt there. "I was never really comfortable with a man before. I kept wondering about all sorts of things."

His mouth brushed tenderly against her ear lobe. "Like what?"

"What does he think of me . . . what does he expect me to do . . . what will he be like afterward."

"I hate to give away any trade secrets, but men think about the same things."

"Are you," she asked, "right now?"

"No," he admitted, clearly as surprised as she. "To tell you the truth, I'm not thinking at all."

Her fingers spread out, encompassing more of him, the nails scratching lightly. "That's nice."

"Hmmm, very."

The deep timbre of his voice made her aware suddenly of how she was arousing him. She made to draw back, only to be stopped by his hand over hers. "Don't. I like you to touch me."

"I like it, too," she admitted. More than she would have thought possible. Judith had never been frigid—exactly—but her relationships with men, what few there had been of them, had not inspired her to think of sex as particularly important. She had come to the conclusion that she was one of those people to whom it simply didn't matter much. The discovery of how wrong she had been astounded her.

Gavin was waking her to a degree of pure wantonness beyond all her expectations. With increasing boldness, she caressed him, spurred on by the husky moans that broke from him and by her growing awareness of her own power.

He seemed to understand that she needed to explore him at her own speed. Lying back against the pillows, he permitted her to do so even as his body grew painfully hard and his breath came in short gasps.

He had been with women more skillful, in a mechanical way, but never had any woman aroused him more. Not even Carrie. The shock of that, compounded by guilt, momentarily froze him.

Judith felt the change in him and looked up. Her hair, golden in the soft light filtering through the windows, fell over her face, partially obscuring it. Her eyes were slumberous and her lips moist and parted. Had the image of her been captured at that moment, it would have been said forever after to represent woman incarnate. Yet there was also a guilelessness about her that stilled the hasty recrimination flowing through Gavin's mind and made him take a deep breath of resolve.

"A man can only stand so much, sweetheart," he said as his hands slid up her arms to take her gently by the shoulders.

Reassured by his evident pleasure, which was so at odds with the brief flash of some other emotion she had felt in him, Judith smiled. Caught in languor of her own making, she was taken by surprise when he turned suddenly and reversed their positions.

Lying beneath him, one of his legs thrown over hers and his fingers loosely twined around her wrists, she knew a moment of the severest doubt. What was she doing in this bed, with this man? Had she forgotten the harsh lessons of the past, not the least of which was her own capacity for self-delusion where matters of the heart were concerned?

"Gavin..."

"Shh," he murmured. "We won't go any faster than you want to."

Oddly the idea that he could so control the pace of what to her seemed to be rapidly spiraling out of control piqued her feminine pride. Had he forgotten so speedily how she had made him moan and gasp?

"Really?" she said with feigned innocence as she raised her hips by the smallest degree, enough for the smooth skin of her belly to rub against his engorged manhood.

"I...uh...wouldn't want to rush you."

"How nice."

They were playing now, and both knew it. Word games, love games, small teasing sallies that men and women who feel truly close to each other have indulged in from time immemorial. For Judith the experience was a complete novelty; for Gavin, a treasure of the past he had thought lost to him forever, instead restored in new and enticing form.

Awareness of that, coupled with the instinctive male need not to lose what he had so unexpectedly found, snapped his hard-fought restraint. The teasing light was gone from his eyes when he lowered his head and claimed her mouth in a kiss of devastating thoroughness. The blatant use of his tongue to evoke what they were shortly to share on an even more intimate level sent shock waves pounding through Judith. She arched against him, her nails digging into his back and a low groan of pure pleasure breaking from her.

The animalistic sound gave way to a low, throaty purr as his hands cupped her small, firm breasts, the thumbs rubbing rhythmically over her aching nipples. Her legs parted and slid around his, the soft skin of her inner thighs brushing against his hardness. She gasped his name as he tore his mouth from her and thirstily suckled her.

The scent of her bath oils mingled with the earthy aromas of musk and sweat as their bodies twined together. Another time they might be able to manage the delights of long, drawn-out lovemaking, but that was beyond them now. Each hungered fiercely for the final joining, the ultimate completion.

When it came, Judith cried out softly. He filled her utterly, moving in long, sure strokes that brought her swiftly to the edge of the precipice, only to hesitate there, held in thrall to his male power, until her own female equivalent reasserted itself and with a sudden urge shattered his taut control.

His final thrust into her was almost painful, so large and demanding was he. But blinding pleasure wiped out any discomfort before it could begin. Never had she experienced anything remotely like the feelings Gavin unleashed. She was lifted out of herself, freed of all physical restraint, her spirit sent soaring. Nothing existed except the man she clung to, the only solid reality in a world turned suddenly to the shattering brilliance of an exploding sun. She chanted his name even as he cried out hers as together they found the furthest reaches of ecstasy.

Much later, when they lay peacefully together on the bed, their heartbeats returned to some semblance of normality, Gavin laughed softly. "The first moment I saw you, I knew it would be like this between us. I thought I was crazy to even imagine it, but no matter how hard I tried, I couldn't get you out of my mind."

She turned over on her side, propping herself up with her chin resting on the palm of one hand, and regarded him with languid confidence. "Did you try very hard?"

"No," he admitted. "There wouldn't have been any point."

Her other hand toyed lightly with the fine whorls of hair on his chest. "That bothers you, doesn't it?"

"That I don't have any self-control where you're concerned? You bet it does." He stroked the curve of her breast, watching with satisfaction as the peak instantly hardened. "My only consolation is that you're in the same boat."

She drew back slightly, though not enough to evade his touch. "You're sure of that?"

His smile was reminiscent of everything they had just shared. "Yes."

She took a playful swat at him, only to have her hand gently caught and held in his. "Don't be angry," he said. "I just don't think we have time for evasions."

Judith had to agree with that. Already she had a painful sense of time passing. She turned away from him, lying flat on the bed and staring up at the ceiling mural with its leering gods and goddesses. "I'm due back in New York next week."

"I know, but a lot could happen between then and now."

She shook her head. "We shouldn't fool ourselves. This is very... temporary."

"A one-night stand?"

"If you like."

"No," he said, abruptly looming over her. "I don't like it at all. What's more, I don't think you do either."

"That's got nothing to do with it. The fact is we have completely separate lives thousands of miles apart."

He cupped her chin, compelling her to look at him. "I won't be in Gregoria forever."

"No, I suppose not, but then where will you be? Paris? Rome? Beijing?"

"Would you believe Washington?"

For the briefest of moments, she allowed herself to hope. Washington wasn't all that bad. An hour away on the shuttle, within easy reach for weekends, holidays... But what was she thinking of? There was far more involved than simply whatever physical distance happened to separate them.

"Don't do this," she murmured. "There's no point lying to ourselves."

"Then let's not. Tell me the truth. Do you want our relationship to continue?"

What did that mean exactly? Seeing him occasionally, making love, perhaps having some small part in his children's lives? Once she would never have settled for any such arrangement. But she had learned that growing older also meant coming to terms with one's limitations. If that was all she could have, damn straight she wanted it.

"I'd like to see you again," she admitted carefully, "but..."

"No buts. We're two intelligent, strong-willed people. We can work it out."

He sounded so certain, when she was anything but. "Aren't you overlooking something?" she asked.

He curled a strand of her hair around his fingers, watching how the light glinted off it. "Your story?"

"Exactly. I would hate to find myself in the position of being accused of sleeping with you in order to get an exclusive."

"Is that why you did it?"

"Of course not!"

"Then why worry? People will say whatever they want to regardless of what we do or don't do."

"You're taking a very cavalier attitude," she said.

"On the contrary. I simply have my priorities straight." He smiled as he bent to her. "Now we're going to work on yours."

Chapter 10

Her priorities—it was as good a term as any—were definitely moving in new and interesting directions by the time she dressed and joined Gavin downstairs.

They had agreed that any attempt at serious discussion in the bedroom would be futile, since no matter what they said or did they ended up making love. Looking at herself in the bathroom mirror, Judith took in the languorous softness of her eyes, the swollen fullness of her mouth, and the telltale blush that made her skin glow and smiled ruefully. She looked like a woman who had been thoroughly loved; moreover, she felt the same way.

Which, she reminded herself as she left the room and walked down the stairs to the main floor, was a singularly dangerous state to be in. This business of wearing two hats—as both Gavin's lover and a journalist responsible for breaking a major story in which he was one of the chief participants—was already proving to be almost more than she could manage. She could imagine all too easily what Sam Wexman would say about it, and about what such a lapse in professional judgment could do to her chances of getting the anchor job.

The funny thing was while she could hear Sam clearly enough in her imagination, she couldn't seem to care much about the havoc her behavior could wreak on her career. That more than anything else brought her up short. For almost a decade, her career had been her life. Everything else had been subordinate to it. It was her shelter and her bulwark, protecting her from other, more personal considerations too painful to confront.

Except now she had to. Gavin all unknowingly had seen to that.

Shadows darkened her eyes as she entered the exotic living room. There was no sign of Gavin, but she did spy a discreet servant flitting down a corridor toward the back of the house and called after him. A brief inquiry elicited the information that lunch was being served on the patio.

She met that news with relief, having been wondering how much more successful they would be concentrating on business in so voluptuous a setting. The rain had stopped while they were too distracted to notice, and the sun shone brilliantly on a bucolic setting of shade trees, flower beds, and emerald-green lawns stretching to the edge of the adjacent forest. The air was washed clean and scented with pine. She breathed it in deeply, hoping to disperse the sensual mists still clinging to her.

Gavin was sitting beside a table set for two. He rose when he caught sight of her, the intimacy of his smile reminding her forcefully of all she had to fear. Dressed in beige linen slacks and an open-necked shirt, with his hair ruffled by the breeze and his chiseled features burnished by the sun, he looked almost unbearably handsome. All too vividly she remembered what lay beneath those casually elegant clothes and how thoroughly she had learned to know his body. Even as he had hers. The soft cotton dress she had chosen to put on was more relaxed and feminine than most of her wardrobe. She had left her legs bare and done nothing with her hair except brush it. Belatedly, she regretted not arraying herself in more appropriate armor.

"I hope you're hungry," he said as he held out her chair for her. "If the smells coming from the kitchen are anything to go by, we're in for a feast."

Actually she was starved. Breakfast seemed about a week ago, and the activity she had indulged in since then had worked up her appetite. She murmured something appropriate but refrained from looking at him any further, evincing instead great interest in the landscape.

"What a pretty garden," she said.

"Perhaps you'd like to take a walk through it later."

"Hmmm. Now, about the story..."

"Couldn't that wait until after lunch?" he asked, offering the basket of warm rolls a waiter had just placed on the table next to a small container of butter curls.

Judith selected one but despite the rumblings of her stomach made no effort to enjoy it. Instead, she said, "I think it's already waited long enough, so if you wouldn't mind, I'd like to get started now." Before he could come up with any other reasons for delay, she drew a small notebook and pencil from the pocket of her dress and set them on the table. "Suppose you start at the beginning, and I'll ask questions as needed."

Gavin cast a longing glance at the seafood cocktail being set before him but patiently refrained from picking up his fork. He nodded to the waiter to pour the wine, waited until the man was gone, then said, "All right. To keep it short and sweet, the only known supply of xanium has been located here in Gregoria, and the United States is determined to secure it for our own use. Delicate diplomatic negotiations are underway to convince His Highness to sign a treaty of friendship."

"So much I had surmised."

"The problem is that we aren't alone in trying to get the xanium. The Russians are involved, of course, but there's also evidence that a European consortium is trying to secure it for themselves."

That was news and Judith raised an eyebrow at it. "A private consortium?"

Gavin paused long enough to take a bite of the seafood, found it delicious, and said, "Probably not. Some of our allies—in this case, I use the word advisedly—would prefer to control the xanium themselves. Really you can't blame them. Western Europe is in something of a cleft stick, trapped between the colliding interests of the U.S. and the U.S.S.R. It's not surprising they've gotten tired of it and want some leverage of their own."

"I suppose they're trying to appeal to Gregory on the grounds that he, too, is a European."

"Exactly, and they have a good case there. Gregory likes Americans well enough, but I know there are times when we just plain baffle him. He feels more comfortable with the British, French, and others like that."

"It sounds as though you think they have the upper hand," she said, making notes.

"Not necessarily. If Gregory had his druthers, he'd stay neutral."

"And sell the xanium to the highest bidder?"

Gavin shot her an appreciative look. "That's the problem. He sees the advantage to the kingdom of a substantial influx of cash, but he's not willing to sacrifice his principles in order to get it. What he'd really like is to share it out at a set price among whoever can use it."

"What's wrong with that?" Judith asked.

Gavin hesitated. He had a problem answering that one. As a man, a member of the human race, and a father concerned with what sort of future his children would have, he thought Gregory's plan had a lot to recommend it. But as a diplomat, he knew it was flawed.

"The difficulty," he said, "is that there's no guarantee everyone would develop a nuclear defense at the same time. If the Soviets got it first, all the rest of us would be extremely vulnerable."

Judith had heard this argument before. She didn't reject it out of hand, but neither could she fully accept it. "Surely something could be arrived at through negotiations...."

Gavin shrugged. "Maybe, maybe not. At any rate, the safest course from our point of view is to convince Gregory to give the U.S. exclusive rights to the xanium."

"And you think you can do that?"

"I don't know," he admitted frankly. "There are...complications."

Judith's hand holding the pencil stilled in its movement over the paper. "What kind?"

"Threats have been made."

"Against Gregory?"

"Worse, against Althea."

"I see..."

"Do you?" he asked, his face suddenly grim. "Gregory loves her. For the first time in his life, he is genuinely devoted to another human being. If the threats were against him, he'd brush them off. But through Althea, he's vulnerable. He can't stand the thought of losing her."

Judith didn't have to wonder at the pain and anger in his voice. He spoke as a man who had lost the woman he loved in a brutal act of terrorism. The bond he must be feeling with Gregory would be acute.

"That's why she's under such tight security?"

He nodded. "You saw the look on his face when she took so long getting back from the stables."

Remembering, Judith frowned. "She doesn't seem to be taking the danger as seriously as he does."

Gavin sat back in his chair and idly twirled his wineglass. "Althea is very young. At her age, we all believe ourselves to be immune from trouble."

She thought about that for a moment, then shook her head. "There's more to it. She's trying to reassure him by showing that she isn't afraid."

"Possibly, but it makes no difference. If they— whoever they are—get to her, we may be sunk."

"You don't know where the threats are coming from?"

He shook his head. "If Gregory had been able to discover that, nothing could keep him from acting. But as it is, he's stymied. And with the wedding only a few days away, Althea will be an increasingly visible target."

"Couldn't the wedding be postponed?"

"Not without arousing a great deal of speculation. For the same reason, it can't be turned into a small, private affair. No, like it or not, Gregory and Althea are stuck firmly in the public eye."

"It sounds as though you expect trouble."

She didn't have to spell out for him what she was thinking; he caught on to it instantly. "And if it happens, you'll be stuck here."

"Which I will hardly appreciate, any more than my network will."

"We made a deal," he reminded her.

"I know, but—"

"Are you trying to back out?"

"Of course not. I'm only saying that if another major story breaks, I would expect you to reevaluate the situation. Naturally, you'd have my word that I wouldn't say anything about the xanium negotiations until they are completed."

"The negotiations are key to anything else that might happen. You could hardly avoid mentioning them."

At least he hadn't suggested that her word wasn't enough. Still, they would have to work something out. It was all very well and good that her career no longer seemed to be taking first place with her; that didn't mean it had vanished completely from her consciousness.

The waiter returned to remove the now-empty plates of seafood salad and replace them with a dish of spinach pasta enrobed in fragrant tomato sauce and succulent bites of anchovy.

"If I stay here very long," Judith said after taking a bite, "I'll be as big as a house."

Gavin smiled quite pleasantly, giving her no warning of what he was about to say. "No you won't. I'll work it off you."

When she blushed, he laughed delightedly, which put a period to any thoughts of serious discussion, at least for the next few minutes. They were content to simply stare into each other's eyes, as lovers are supposed to, until dessert arrived.

Over coffee and crisp apple tart, Judith made a valiant effort to return to the matter at hand. "Gavin, if something happens to Althea, you must see that I can't stay here and wait it out. It would be worth my head back in New York to do that."

After a moment's consideration he said, "All right, I'll make you another deal."

"You sound like Monty Hall."

"Back when I was in training at the State Department, that show was all we watched. Wouldn't miss it."

Despite herself, Judith laughed. "Is that how you see diplomacy, people dressed up in funny outfits trying to pick the right door?"

He took a sip of his espresso and looked at her thoughtfully. "Sometimes that's exactly how it is."

"I could do an interesting story along those lines."

"Just don't mention my name."

"How could I when I've forgotten it already?"

He finished the apple tart and looked at the remains of hers with unmistakable interest. "Fresh, that's what you are."

"Yep, uppity too." With a flourish, she finished the last bite and sat back, replete. "I'm stuffed. How about that walk?"

They left the patio and strolled along a cinder path that led through the gardens. Behind a yew hedge that topped both their heads, they found a secluded glade complete with gazebo. From its shaded benches, they watched a pair of graceful deer nibbling their way up the hillside. A stork flew overhead, undoubtedly making for the city, where he and his like nested on unused chimneys.

Judith was very tempted to forget everything else that might be on her mind and simply concentrate on the beauty of her surroundings, but the niggling voice of conscience stopped her. "About that deal you mentioned," she said.

Gavin had his head back, his eyes closed to the sun. He seemed almost asleep, but the impression was deceptive. In fact, his mind was working in hyperdrive. "If something does happen, I'll make sure you know about it."

"That's not quite the same as saying I'll be able to cover it."

He straightened, his face a mask she could not read. She had the sudden sense of him moving away from her, down some path she could not follow; it was an experience that hurt as much as it baffled.

"If something does happen," he said slowly, "it will be very dangerous."

"I'm used to that."

"Don't brush it off so lightly!" He rose suddenly, his hands thrust into his pockets, his jaw set. "Do I have to spell it out for you? I don't want you to be threatened."

She understood, or at least she thought she did, and that understanding astounded her. Of course Gavin would not want to see anyone willfully endangered, but the ferocity—there was no other word for it—with which he objected to her being placed in a situation that might turn nasty suggested he had more at stake than he was quite willing to acknowledge.

Again she thought of Carrie, the beloved wife who had died violently, and told herself not to jump to conclusions.

"All right," she said quietly, "you'll make sure I know what's going on and we'll take it from there." Before he could reply, she reached for his hand. "In the meantime, let's enjoy what we have."

He was willing enough to be persuaded. Both of them lived in such a high-pressure world, with such little time to even notice the beauties of life, let alone appreciate them, that their stay at the "hunting" lodge was a stolen interlude of the rarest sort.

Hand in hand they wandered along a path that led them deep into the pine forest. There, in the cool shadows of the arching trees, they watched squirrels flit from branch to branch, spied several foxes creeping after their prey, and were even fortunate enough to see one of the wild horses for which Gregoria was renowned.

"They're said to descend from the mounts brought here by the first Gregory," Gavin explained, softly so as not to startle the great stallion. "Several got loose, and out of gratitude for their service, no effort was made to recapture them. To this day, their descendants roam these hills."

"He's magnificent," Judith murmured, awestruck by the powerful animal's proud strength. As she watched, a lovely chestnut mare appeared over the rise of the hill. The stallion raised his head, looked at her and whinnied softly. The mare obeyed the summons, and together they disappeared over the farthest rise.

Gavin looked at Judith and said, "How about going back to the lodge?"

Feeling more deliciously wicked than she ever had in her life, she asked, "What's wrong with right here?"

His eyes fell on the soft piles of needles spread out at their feet. A slow smile made his intentions radiantly clear. "Nothing that I can see."

They sank together onto the welcoming ground. Slowly they undressed each other as the soft breeze fluttered over them and distant birds cooed faintly. For Judith the scene was so lovely as to be all but painful. Even as it unfolded, she warned herself to store every precious detail in her memory against a future that promised by comparison to be no more than barren.

Gavin had much the same thought, except that in his case he was determined to hold on to what he had found, a treasure that with each passing moment was revealing herself to be even lovelier than he had first suspected.

In the shadows cast by the pine trees, her skin was ivory and gold. The rounded softness of her body in counterpoint with the angular lines of the forest made her like a rare jewel deliberately placed in a contrasting setting so as to heighten every aspect of her beauty.

Not that any such exaggeration was needed. Entranced by her, Gavin knelt as though to an icon. Tenderly, almost suppliantly, he stroked her from the hollow between her collarbones down between her swelling breasts to the curve of her belly and beyond. She trembled under his touch, reaching to caress him in turn.

This time their lovemaking was slower and more deliberately drawn out. With the first frantic urgency quenched, they were able to lead each other higher and higher toward a shimmering peak of pleasure that, when it was at last attained, left them both drained yet replenished.

Side by side, they lay on the cool ground, their hands clasped. Gavin broke the silence first.

"Don't talk to me about this being temporary," he said. "I would rather have never met you at all than to have to say goodbye to you in a few days." That wasn't quite true; whatever happened, he would always cherish the time he had had with her. But he was greedy, an emotion fueled by the conviction deep inside that fate had cheated him once and must not be allowed to do so again.

"There's so much to consider," she hedged. Gathering her courage, she added, "Your children, for instance."

He turned on his side, looking at her. "Why should that be a problem?"

"They might not like me."

Gavin laughed and touched her cheek gently. "Don't be silly. They'll love you."

Her heart jerked at that thought. When she remained silent, he said, "Unless . . . Is it that you don't like kids?"

"No, not at all. I just don't have much experience with them."

"That's right. You don't have any of your own, do you?"

She averted her eyes. "You know I've never been married."

"Some women don't let that bother them."

"It would me."

There was something in her silence, in the way she scrupulously avoided looking at him, that made Gavin wonder if he had inadvertently tripped over a sensitive topic. He knew that some women, when they passed thirty, started to hear a biological clock ticking, making them question whether they had made the right decision in postponing childbearing and possibly also marriage in favor of their careers. It hadn't occurred to him that Judith might be having such doubts, but he could come up with no other explanation for her sudden withdrawal.

Meaning to reassure her, he said, "You're certainly still young enough to have children."

She cast him a look through the veil of her lashes. "Tell me about yours. You love them very much, don't you?"

Aware though he was that she had deliberately sidestepped the possibility of future motherhood, he did not pursue it. There would be time enough for that later, when circumstances calmed down and they could think of the future. It pleased him to look forward to that day, which, hopefully, was not too far off. He considered what Jessie and Davey would make of her and decided that she would have little trouble winning their hearts.

"I don't know what I'd do without my kids," he admitted without embarrassment. "I can be embroiled in the worst crisis, worn out and really dragging, and just a few minutes with them will recharge me. Which is not to say," he added with a grin, "that they can't be holy terrors when they want to be."

"I'd love to meet them," Judith said softly.

"As soon as things settle down," he promised, "we'll all get together."

His obvious eagerness for her to meet his children warmed her, but it also raised future problems that she couldn't bear to think of just then. Not with the sun warming their naked bodies, the soft breeze caressing them, and time seemingly content to stand still at the pleasure of lovers lost in a world of their own making.

Resolutely locking her fears away in a distant corner of her mind, she reached out to him.

Chapter 11

Shortly before dusk they returned to the lodge, where Gavin broke the news that he had to go back to the capital that night. "I don't want to leave you," he said frankly, "but I must meet with Gregory again. He's under increasing pressure from the Soviets and the Europeans." Prudence dictated that he not tell her there had also been another warning from the terrorists.

"I understand," Judith said, which was true even though she deeply regretted his departure. So long as he was still there, she could refrain from thinking too much about their relationship and where it might or might not be leading. Left alone, she had no doubt her thoughts would demand to be heard.

"I'll try to get back tomorrow," he said. "If there's any problem, I'll call."

She smiled through her concern. "This will give me a chance to get started on my story."

He set down the overnight bag he had been packing and came to where she sat in the window seat of his bedroom with her legs curled up beneath her and a deliberately disengaged expression on her face. Halting very close to her, he asked, "Does that mean you won't miss me?"

"Well . . . I will be very busy."

He laughed tenderly and laid his hands on her shoulders, drawing her upward to him. "Liar. You'll be going as crazy as I will."

"Has anyone ever told you that you're a touch too confident?"

"As a matter of fact, I'm known for my uncanny ability to accurately judge any situation."

"Modest, too."

"Not around you, sweetheart."

That was food for thought after he had left. The idea that a man might feel at all self-conscious about even the most intimate lovemaking had never occurred to Judith. She had simply presumed that men did not experience the same reticence women did. And some undoubtedly did not. But a man like Gavin— private, discerning, idealistic—might well hesitate to share so much of himself. That he had not felt self-conscious with her told her almost more than she wanted to know.

Despite her bold assertion, her attempts at getting started on the story met with little success. After a solitary dinner served by the virtually invisible staff, she went up to bed intending to read for a while and make it an early night.

If a tired body had been enough, she would have fallen asleep the moment her head touched the pillow. The exertions of the last two days—delightful though they had been—had worn her out, and she longed for dreamless rest. It was not to be hers, however, as she tossed and turned, finally giving up toward midnight and going to stare out the window at the moon-dappled landscape.

Her mind was on Gavin, wondering what he was doing and whether he was thinking of her, when a shadow flitting down the garden path caught her eye. Her first guess was that she had spied some nocturnal predator, except that none she could think of were tall and slender, and only one she knew of walked on two legs.

Considering whether or not to alert the servants, she watched as the man—so his silhouette revealed him to be—scampered over a yew bush, paused to get his bearings and headed toward the lodge. In another moment he would be lost from sight.

Unhesitantly, Judith stepped out onto the balcony beyond her room, took a quick glance at the ground, which after all did not look so very far away, and swung herself over the side. The latticework of the balcony afforded convenient hand-holds, and she was able to lower herself to within a few feet of the ground before letting go.

When she had caught her breath, she took off after the intruder, finding him intent on jimmying a window of the kitchen. She waited until he managed it and climbed inside, then carefully peered after him.

The figure revealed by the light of the open refrigerator was all too familiar. It took her barely a moment to place him, and when she did all thought of discretion fled. "Jim West! What on earth are you doing?"

Caught in the act of chomping on a chicken leg, he turned and stared at her dumbly. Only belatedly did he think to remove the object from his mouth and give her a knowing smile. "So I was right. You are here."

"Are you out of your mind?" she demanded, reaching through the window to unlatch the kitchen door. A moment later she was inside and glaring at him. "You're lucky no one took a shot at you."

West's smile faded. He helped himself to a cold bottle of beer and drank it almost in one swallow before he said, "Why do you think I didn't come out earlier? Believe me, honey, it was no picnic hiding out in the woods since yesterday."

"You followed us," Judith said. "There's no other way you could have found this place."

"Damn straight I did. I know you don't think much of me, but if there's one thing I've learned it's how to stay on the trail of a story. And what I smelled between you and Penderast was too good to miss."

Disgusted as much by his choice of words as by his arrogance, Judith said, "What's the matter, West? You get scared you'd have to go home empty-handed and decide to manufacture a little dirt instead?"

"You mean about you and God's gift to women shacking up together in this little love nest?" He shrugged dismissively. "Who cares? No, I've got bigger fish to fry."

Much as she would have liked to let that pass if only to annoy him, she felt driven to ask, "Such as?"

"Why an ambitious newswoman zeroing in on the anchor chair walks away from an assignment to have a little fling. That's out of character, sweetheart. I don't care how much you and Penderast have the hots for each other; I don't see you putting a good time in bed ahead of your career."

"Your vocabulary could use improvement, West. It's on the level of a fourteen-year-old's."

An ugly look crossed his face. "Let me give you a piece of advice. Don't get nasty with me. I'm holding all the cards."

"Oh, really? And just what game do you imagine we're playing?"

"It's called power, honey. The only game that counts. Good King Gregory is finding out that a little is a dangerous thing."

"I have no idea what you're talking about."

His response was short and explicit. "Then let me spell it out for you. X-a-n-i-u-m. Sound familiar?"

Judith walked farther into the kitchen, shut the refrigerator door he had carelessly left open, and said, "Suppose we sit down and talk."

"That's more like it. But before we do, how about fixing me something more to eat? I'm starved."

Judith gritted her teeth and did as he bade. She knew he was deliberately provoking her, but she refused to let him see that she minded. Whatever he was up to, she wouldn't find out by getting his back up.

After she had set a plate of sandwiches in front of him, along with a stein of beer, she took a seat on the other side of the table, prepared to wait until he had eaten his fill. Unfortunately, West was of the two-birds-with-one-stone school and proceeded to regale her with his brilliancy, munching all the while.

Bits of bread and meat clung to his teeth as he expounded on how he had sniffed out the real story of what was happening in Gregoria. "I met some chaps in a bar the other night and they started telling me about..."

Judith almost missed the next part of what he had to say. She despised Americans abroad who affected anglicisms, and would have told him so if he hadn't gone blissfully on.

"They started telling me about how these geologists had stopped by Gregoria on a little holiday and stumbled across what everyone and his brother has been looking for since those guys at M.I.T. made their discovery."

"They told you this?" she repeated dubiously.

"Well, not exactly. Fact is they'd had quite a lot to drink and were shooting their mouths off. I just happened to be close enough to hear."

Judith didn't doubt it. West seemed to have a positive talent for worming his way in where he wasn't supposed to be.

"So you heard about the xanium...."

"And about the threats against Althea. Pretty smart, that. Hit old Gregory where it hurts the most."

"They talked about the threats?"

"You hard of hearing or something? That's what I said."

Which put an entirely different complexion on the matter. It was conceivable, if only barely, that someone might innocently have found out about the xanium discovery and had the bad luck to talk about it in West's presence. But the only people she could imagine knowing about the threats against Althea were either Gregorian security personnel, who she doubted got drunk and shot off their mouths in bars, and the terrorists themselves.

"Jim, this could be really important. Do you remember anything else about those men—what they looked like, for instance?"

"Maybe. What if I do?"

"Then you have to tell the authorities!" she exclaimed. "Maybe they can catch them before they do any harm."

"And maybe being a nice guy will get the story ripped out from under me."

"You can't think of that! There's a life involved here. Althea could be seriously hurt, or even worse." She was appalled by his callousness, but sadly enough not surprised by it. As short a time as she had known him, she already realized that he was single-minded in his ambition and had absolutely no qualms about how he achieved it.

"Anyway," he went on, blissfully unaware of her disgust, "I did a little sniffing around and figured out that you'd made some kind of deal with Penderast to give you an exclusive on the story. Pretty smart, I've got to admit."

"I'm so glad you approve," she said icily.

"I sure do, honey—provided, of course, that you cut me in."

"I don't see how I can do that."

West burped, shoved his empty plate aside, and said, "You don't have much choice. I'm still missing a few pieces, but I can go with the story I've got if I have to."

"Your network won't touch it without all the pieces *and* collaboration."

"Could be, but I can still get it out. Not everyone's so scrupulous."

That was sadly true. It wouldn't take West long to find some outlet for the story, no matter how incomplete it was or how much damage it could do to national security.

"And," he added, "I don't have to tell you what will happen if the story leaks before the negotiations are completed."

"Gregory is likely to pick any other option over giving the U.S. control of the xanium."

He smiled wolfishly. "Who says blondes are dumb? You got it on one."

By dint of extraordinary personal discipline, Judith managed to keep her temper. She gave him a long, slow smile that would have chilled the blood of anyone who knew her at all well and said, "So you want my help on the story?"

"I wouldn't put it that way. What I'm offering you is an opportunity to combine forces."

"Sorry, I misunderstood. Of course, you realize that I can't divulge any information to you without the approval of my source."

"You mean Penderast?" West said. "He shouldn't be any problem."

The look he gave her made it clear why he believed that. He surmised that she and Gavin were lovers and that she should be able to use sex to get him to agree to whatever she wanted.

"We'll see." She rose stiffly, anxious to put as much distance between them as she could before she exploded. "If you'll excuse me, I'm going to get some sleep."

"What about me?"

She looked back disinterestedly. "I can hardly present you to the staff as a guest. They'd know in a second that something was wrong and report you."

"Well, I sure as hell don't plan to sleep outside again tonight," he snarled.

Judith thought for a moment. "There's an old shed at the edge of the field near the forest. You could sleep there."

"I've got a better idea." He stood up and came toward her, his eyes raking her slender figure through the pajamas she wore. "Let's share your room."

"No, thanks."

"Hey, why not? We're going to be working together, so we might as well get to be friends."

Judith had no doubt how he envisioned their "friendship." She wasted no time disabusing him of the notion. "I'm not interested."

The look that crossed his face was ugly and dangerous. "That's too bad. You don't know what you're missing."

"My loss." She turned again to leave, only to be stopped by his hand on her shoulder. "You don't have any stupid ideas about getting in touch with Penderast and blowing the whistle on me, do you?"

Since this was exactly what she was thinking of doing, Judith was momentarily taken aback. But she managed to conceal her surprise behind an impenetrable smile. "You worry too much, Jim. Why would I risk blowing a top-notch story just to do Gavin a favor?"

"Yeah . . ." he said slowly, "why would you?"

Before he could pursue the subject any further, she looked at her arm pointedly. "I'll say good-night, then."

Reluctantly, he let her go. His confidence was back in place and he decided to make one more try. "You know you'll change your mind about us."

"Anything's possible," she said, though she knew that in this case it most certainly wasn't. Back in the hall, with the kitchen door safely closed behind her, she gave vent to her anger with a single, well-chosen mutter. That done, she turned her mind to the problem of getting in touch with Gavin.

There had to be a phone somewhere in the lodge, but she had yet to see it. There were jacks in the bedrooms, but whatever phones might have been connected to them had been removed. It occurred to her that Gavin would have taken steps to prevent her from getting in touch with Sam Wexman at the first opportunity as soon as she had the story. She was hurt that he hadn't trusted her more, but more important, she was vexed that she had to search for some way to reach him.

It took her half an hour, but she eventually found it. An old-fashioned black dial phone was hidden away in a coat closet underneath the stairs. There was no directory within sight, and she realized with an impatient grumble that she had no idea of the number of the American embassy. But she needn't have worried. Picking up the receiver was enough to prompt a series of clicks, at the end of which an operator offered to assist her.

Moments later she had reached the duty officer at the embassy and was explaining that she urgently had to speak with Ambassador Penderast.

"I'm sorry, miss," the man said. "We're closed for the night. Perhaps you would like to call back tomorrow and speak with one of the attaches."

"You don't understand. This is an emergency and I must speak with the ambassador. If you'll just tell him I'm on the phone, I'm sure he'll—"

"One moment, miss," the man said, interrupting her before she could finish. What followed were in fact many frustrating minutes of delay before at last another male voice said, "May I help you?"

"That depends," Judith said caustically. "I must speak with Ambassador Penderast."

"The ambassador is not available. This is his aide. If you will tell me what the problem is . . ."

Judith was tempted, but she had no idea if the man really was who he said he was, much less if he would understand and act on her information. "I'm sorry, but I can't. It's confidential."

"I assure you, miss, that if you will simply tell me what the problem is, I will see that it is handled properly."

Pushed to the wall, Judith took the only approach she felt certain would get her through to Gavin. "All right, will you kindly tell the ambassador that the lady he recently spent the night with is in trouble and has to speak to him at once?"

An endless silence followed, interrupted at last by a nervous cough. "Ah . . . would you hold on, miss?"

Judith sighed and resigned herself to another long wait. Minutes ticked by. She rubbed the back of her neck where the muscles had tensed and stared around the closet. It was filled with the usual detritus that seems to accumulate under stairs: anonymous boxes, old pictures in dusty frames, yellowed newspapers, unmatched shoes. The sheer ordinariness of such a place in the midst of an exotic love nest amused her. She was feeling marginally better when Gavin at last came on the line.

"I want you to know," he said without preamble, "that my stock has just gone up quite a bit with my aide."

Judith laughed softly. "Because he thinks you've been having a wild fling?"

"Exactly. Now, what's this about trouble?"

Briefly she told him about West. He cursed softly. "Damn it, I should have anticipated something like that. Where is he now?"

"If he took my advice, he's heading for that old shed to get some sleep."

Gavin was doubtful about that. "Make sure you look under your bed before you get in it. The guy sounds like a real creep."

"Well put, but unfortunately there's more. He knows Althea's in danger; moreover, he's seen the terrorists."

"Are you sure about that?" Gavin demanded tensely.

"Not a hundred percent. With West there's never any way to tell whether he's on the level or just trying to sound important. But I think there's a good chance he really did see them. I tried to convince him to give the authorities descriptions, but he refused."

"He'll change his mind," Gavin said ominously.

Judith didn't ask how he could be so sure; she really didn't want to know. Instead she was content to leave the matter in his hands.

"I'll arrange for a security team to get out there right away," he said. "Until then, I'd appreciate it if you'd stay inside. Wake the servants and tell them I'm concerned about possible intruders. They'll know what to do."

"All right," she said, not questioning why she was so willing to follow his instructions.

The servants were equally eager to do so. Barely had she found their rooms, in a separate building some little distance from the main lodge, and told them what Gavin had said than they swiftly assured her that they would see to everything.

Wooden shutters were secured over the windows and doors were bolted. Several of the young footmen were armed with hunting rifles and posted outside to stand guard. The efficiency of the preparations, and particularly the presence of weapons, made Judith realize that Gavin had not chosen the lodge only for its aesthetic qualities. She had the distinct impression that the staff was trained for a good deal more than simply providing discreet service to lovers.

Feeling distinctly *de trop*, she withdrew to her room to dress and await developments. They weren't long in coming. Before she had barely begun mulling over what had happened, she heard the sounds of several cars pulling up in front. Through the slats of the shutters across her windows, she saw eight large men emerge and identify themselves to the guards. Half the group then went inside while the others fanned out over the property.

As she descended the stairs, an older, gray-haired man with the look of a retired football player who had stayed in excellent shape, stepped forward to greet her. "Miss Fairchild, I am William Berdot from Internal Security. Ambassador Penderast told me of your unexpected guest, but I would like to go over the details with you."

"Of course," she said, indicating the way to the living room.

To give Berdot credit, he managed to keep a straight face when confronted with the exotic decorations. Or perhaps he simply wasn't surprised by them. Whichever the case, he was all business as he went over everything with her that Jim West had said and done.

"Whatever information he could give us about the appearance of the terrorists could be invaluable," Berdot said when she had finished.

"I'm afraid he doesn't intend to cooperate."

The security man gave her a smile that held not a shred of humor. "Perhaps we can convince Mr. West to change his mind."

"Ambassador Penderast said something similar; however, it wouldn't do to forget that West has access to powerful media. He could be . . . troublesome."

Berdot inclined his head gravely. "Your concern is appreciated, but be assured that we will take every precaution to see to it that he does not."

Judith didn't like the sound of that. She had only disgust for West and what he was trying to pull, but visions of him disappearing into some medieval dungeon never to be heard from again worried her nonetheless.

Barely had she begun to imagine the worst than common sense took over and she told herself that as angry as Gavin might be, he would never permit an American citizen to be mistreated. Threatened and intimidated, possibly, but not actually harmed. Under the circumstances, she had to agree that the rules should be bent just a bit to get to the bottom of whatever West knew.

But that would have to wait, it became clear when a grim-faced security man stuck his head in the door and exchanged a few tense words with Berdot.

"Is there a problem?" Judith asked when they were alone again.

Berdot was lost in thought for a moment; he had to pull himself back before he could answer her. "I am afraid so. My men went out to the shed. West is not there."

"Perhaps he decided not to take my advice and is hiding somewhere in the woods."

"I think not. There are signs that a struggle took place there quite recently."

"But how...?"

"Unfortunately, it is only too simple. West followed you here; there was nothing to prevent the terrorists from following him. In fact, they may have simply used him for that purpose."

"And now he's in their hands." Much as she disliked him, she was horrified by that thought.

Berdot shrugged. "We will try to find him, of course. There is a trail of sorts, but to follow it in the dark is impossible. It will have to wait until morning, and by then they will be well away."

"You don't think they'd kill him, do you?"

"If he has served his purpose for them, certainly they will." He looked at her directly. "These are extremely unpleasant people, Miss Fairchild. They will do anything to achieve their objectives. Anything at all."

Chapter 12

After that there was no question of Judith remaining at the lodge. While Berdot and the others waited, she packed her belongings, made sure that she had all her notes, and took a last, quick look around the room where she and Gavin had made love.

Telling herself that there would be other times for them, she tried to shake off the ominous feeling that had settled over her as soon as she learned of West's disappearance. She couldn't quite manage to do this, however, before it was time to leave.

The drive back to the capital was made largely in silence. Berdot sat beside her in the back seat of one of the two cars. Two other security men were in front, and two followed. The remainder had been left at the lodge to search for clues and to follow the trail from the shed at first light.

Judith was too weary and preoccupied to even attempt conversation, and Berdot showed no inclination to do so. Occasionally there were static bursts from the two-way radio that relayed information in coded phrases she could not understand; otherwise it was quiet enough for her to doze off.

She woke with a jerk as the car pulled up at the rear entrance of the American embassy. She was swiftly ushered through a door that led into the kitchens, empty at this hour, with their stainless steel stoves and refrigerators gleaming darkly. Beyond them was a narrow hallway and a staircase that led up to the second floor, where Gavin had his quarters.

He was conferring with a young, sandy-haired man who was apparently his aide when he caught sight of her. A relieved smile flashed across his rugged features as he held out his arms to her.

"Judith, I'm so glad you're here."

She went to him and without hesitation was enfolded in his embrace. What the aide made of that, or for that matter what the watching security men thought, was inconsequential to them both. All that mattered was the comfort of being close to each other once again.

When at last he reluctantly stood back from her he asked, "Are you all right?"

She assured him swiftly that she was, but the doubtful look in his eyes made it clear that he had understood more about her encounter with West than she had spelled out for him. There was an underlying note of protectiveness in the way he held her arm as he led her over to the couch that struck some primal chord of femininity within her. For the first time in her life, she understood and was pleased by a man's claiming of her as his own.

"Ask the steward on duty to bring us some coffee," Gavin instructed the aide. "Berdot, my thanks for your assistance."

The security man nodded. "Our pleasure. Now, if you will excuse me, I must get back to the palace."

Left alone, Gavin sat down beside her on the couch and said quietly, "It's been a hell of a night."

"I can imagine." He looked so tired, yet he still exuded that aura of strength and confidence that was second nature to him. She did not doubt that he would go on, pushing himself to the absolute limit, until he dropped. A sudden instinctive need to take care of him rose within her. "Have you had anything to eat recently?"

She thought he hadn't heard her as he ran a hand through his hair distractedly, but finally he said, "Food? No, I hadn't thought of it. Are you hungry?"

She wasn't but had no intention of telling him that. When the steward arrived with a silver coffee service and two cups, she said, "Could you also see about some soup and sandwiches? The ambassador hasn't eaten."

He inclined his head in acknowledgment of her instructions and went away again. Judith poured two cups of the aromatic brew and handed one to Gavin. He took it and sipped absently, his mind clearly elsewhere.

"I really thought you would be safe at the lodge," he said when he had set the cup back down.

Judith was surprised that her security seemed to be so paramount in his mind. Especially when she was sitting right beside him, obviously safe and sound. "There was no harm done," she said reassuringly.

"But there could have been." Unexpectedly, he slammed a clenched fist into the palm of his hand. "Damn it, something has to be done to stop those people. Until they are, every one of us is a hostage to our own fears."

His vehemence and the rage she sensed behind it worried her. Above all, he needed to be calm and controlled in the face of this crisis. Yet at that instant he seemed anything but. "They'll be caught," she said softly. "I'm sure of that."

"Are you? They've gotten away with similar actions time and again in the past. They gloat over our inability to catch and hold them. We're fools in their eyes, and I can't say I blame them for thinking that way."

"But some terrorists have been caught," she said, "and punished. They don't all get away."

"Too many do." He turned away from her, but not before she saw the sudden flash of pain that gripped his features.

Laying a gentle hand on his arm, she said, "Gavin, the ones who killed Carrie, did they escape?"

He nodded and said huskily, "Them and plenty of others. But not this time. Damn it, this time they won't get away."

Judith prayed he was right, if only because of what it would do to his spirit to have the perpetrators of such atrocities walk away a second time. She remembered the look she had seen on Gavin's face as he watched Gregory and Althea in the garden behind the castle. He understood their love for each other, had experienced a similar joy himself, and was determined that theirs would not end as tragically. Highly professional and disciplined though he clearly was, his mission to Gregoria had turned brutally personal. The stakes were his very belief in a world where, despite the worst brutality, there was still hope for a better future.

Gently stroking the back of his neck, she said, "You should get some rest." When he started to shake his head, she added firmly, "You won't be any good to anyone if you're exhausted. At least lie down for a little while. When the food comes, I'll bring it in to you."

"All right," he agreed slowly, "but stay with me."

She could hardly resist such an appeal. Especially not when everything in her heart cried out to be with him.

The room he led her to was large and elegantly furnished with choice pieces of early American furniture and several primitive portraits that would not have looked out of place in the finest museum. It had a comfortably lived-in appearance with a stack of books on the bedside table and a pair of slippers left beneath a round mahogany table where Gavin had apparently been working.

With his help, she folded back the crewel work bedspread, which matched the hangings of the four-poster bed. He did the chore matter-of-factly, which reminded her that he was far removed from any undomesticated bachelor days. This was a man who had loved deeply, who had treasured his marriage, and who adored the children who were the product of it.

He was strong, stable and secure, not at all like so many of the men she had met in the past who blanched at the mere thought of commitment and fled in horror from responsibility. Those men had been little more than children themselves, and Judith had wanted nothing to do with them. Gavin, for all that he needed comforting, was anything but.

They lay down on the bed together, fully dressed except for their shoes. Gavin put an arm around her and drew her close. Judith had very little experience with snuggling; her parents had not been particularly demonstrative, and there had been no opportunity in what had passed for her love life to share such tenderness. But to Gavin it was automatic. He stroked her hair gently as the warmth of his body slowly drove away the chill that had clung to her since the events at the lodge.

"This is very nice," Judith murmured.

"Hmmm, your hair smells good."

"It's my shampoo—lemony."

"No," he said drowsily, "it's you."

She saw no reason to dispute him, content instead to let her eyes drift shut while she managed to remain alert for the sound of the steward in the living room. When she heard him, she slipped out of Gavin's embrace and padded to the door.

If the young man was surprised to see her emerge barefoot and slightly disheveled from the Ambassador's bedroom, he didn't show it. With a whispered thank you, Judith took the tray from him. Gavin was sleeping deeply when she returned. She felt badly about waking him and was debating whether or not to do so when he opened his eyes, looked at the tray, and sat up.

"Is that vegetable soup I smell?" he asked.

"Seems to be." She set the food carefully on the bed. There were thick roast beef and ham sandwiches on whole-wheat bread, individual tureens of rich, chunky soup, a stoneware pitcher of milk, and a platter of frosted brownies studded with walnuts.

"Not bad for a spur-of-the-moment meal," she said after savoring a spoonful of the soup. It was flavored with basil and the merest hint of Tabasco sauce, and well laced with golden streams of butter. They both devoured it in appreciative silence, along with most of the sandwiches and a good portion of the brownies.

Judith was biting into her second of the rich chocolaty treats when Gavin grinned at her. "I thought you weren't hungry."

"I changed my mind."

"Women's prerogative," he said.

"Man's, too."

Their eyes met. "No," he said, "not always. Some things can't be changed. They just are, right from the beginning, and the wise person knows it."

They finished the food without further comment. Gavin helped her clear up even to the extent of brushing the crumbs from the bed. Side by side once again, her head cradled on his chest, they drifted into sleep.

Judith woke a short time later. She was tired, but too tense to rest well. Afraid that she might disturb Gavin, she slipped out of the room and curled up on the living room couch.

It was getting on for dawn. Faint gray light streaked the sky beyond the casement windows. She heard the creak of wagon wheels on the street below and the clatter of horses' hooves.

For an hour or so she worked on her notes, writing down everything she remembered West saying and everything that had happened since. Or almost everything. She saw no reason to mention the meal in Gavin's bedroom, since the purpose of the notes was to jog her memory and she was hardly likely to forget that.

She had just finished and was sitting with her eyes closed moving her head from side to side to ease the tension in her shoulders when she heard the door of the living room open. A little girl with long chestnut hair and large blue eyes peered in.

"Oh," she said softly, "hello."

Judith straightened on the couch. "Hello. Want to come in?"

The little girl nodded. "I'm looking for my father."

Despite the child's delicate prettiness, there was no mistaking who she was. Gavin's directness shone out of eyes that, while not the same color as his, were equally perceptive. "He's asleep, but I think he'll be awake soon. By the way, I'm Judith Fairchild, a friend of your father's." At least that description was true, though it hardly expressed the totality of their relationship.

The child held out her hand gravely. "I'm Jessica, but everyone calls me Jessie." She sat down on the couch beside Judith and regarded her with the steady curiosity of a child who senses that here is someone important. "Have you known Daddy very long?"

"Uh...no, only a few days." And please don't let the child ask how they could have become friends in such a short time.

"Do you like him a lot?"

"Yes, he's...very nice. You have a brother, don't you?" Anything to deflect her curiosity.

Jessie nodded. "Davey. He's five. I'm eight. Do you have children?"

It seemed as though everyone was asking her that these days. "No, I'm sorry to say that I don't." At that moment, looking at the lovely, intelligent little girl, she was sorrier than she had ever been.

"Someday I'll have children," Jessie said confidently. "But not until I'm much older and have done a lot of things. At least that's what Daddy says."

"I'm sure he's right. Do you know what sorts of things you'd like to do?" Please let her already have very complicated and well-developed career plans that she loves to talk about.

"No, but I think I want to be either an astronaut or a doctor."

"Maybe you could be both. If people start living in space colonies, they'll need doctors."

Jessie thought about that for a moment, clearly taken with the idea. But not so much so that she lost interest in Judith. "What kind of work do you do?"

"I'm a reporter on television."

A look of concern flitted across the child's face. "Uh-oh, maybe I shouldn't be talking to you."

"Why do you say that?"

"Because Daddy told us once that we shouldn't talk to reporters about stuff we hear around here. He said the best thing was not to say anything to them."

Before Judith could think of a suitable reply to that, she was saved by a voice from the bedroom doorway. "That's all right, honey," Gavin said. "You can talk with Miss Fairchild. She's a friend of mine."

The little girl ran to him, gave him a hug, and said, "That's what she told me. I'm glad it's true. She's very nice and pretty."

Gavin laughed as much at what his daughter had said as at Judith's sudden blush. "Yes, she certainly is. Did you and Davey behave yourselves while I was gone?"

"Sure, we're always good."

"I don't know about that." With a hand on his daughter's shoulder, he strolled across the room to join Judith on the couch. Jessie remained perched beside him, looking carefully from one adult to the other.

"Weren't you tired?" he asked Judith quietly.

She nodded. "But I have trouble sleeping when there's too much on my mind."

"It would be a good idea to have a nap later."

"Yes . . . well, I'll see how things go."

Gavin seemed perfectly at ease with the intimacy of their discussion, but Judith was not. She kept glancing at Jessie, wondering how much the child was taking in.

Apparently a great deal, for the little girl did not hesitate to ask, "Is Miss Fairchild staying here?"

Before Judith could respond, Gavin said, "Yes, she is. Where's Davey got to? I'd like Judith to meet him, too."

Jessie wrinkled her nose. "He went out in the garden this morning right after Miss Schultz got him dressed and he got all muddy, so she had to give him another bath." With a satisfied grin, she added, "Miss Schultz says he's the dirtiest little boy she's ever seen."

"While you, on the other hand," Gavin said teasingly, "are a little paragon."

"What's paragon mean?" Jessie asked.

"Perfect."

"Well . . . I suppose I could be, if that was what I happened to want to be." She bounced off the arm of the couch and headed for the door. "I have to go to class now. See you later?" She looked at Judith hopefully.

"Sure you will," her father told her. "Miss Fairchild will be here for a while."

Jessie nodded her pleasure at that and hurried off. When she was gone, Judith said, "She's a beautiful child. You've done a wonderful job."

"Thanks," Gavin said. "There were days when I wondered how I'd ever manage, but nothing I've done has ever been more satisfying."

"Not even negotiating treaties and preventing wars?" she asked only half-facetiously.

He shook his head firmly. "No, nothing. I don't think I could ever have worked so hard to build a future without having kids to remind me why it was so important."

"It is too easy to think only of the present," Judith agreed thoughtfully. She had been guilty of that herself, at least so far as her personal life went. Perhaps because it was always too painful to think ahead to what might be.

It startled her to realize how bleakly she had viewed her future apart from her career. She had carefully kept that truth from herself, understanding instinctively that she could not deal with it. In many ways, her difficulty in doing so had not changed. But having Gavin come into her life had given her strong motivation to admit that she hurt inside for all she could not have. Perhaps that was a first step toward dealing with the problem.

"Judith," Gavin said gently, "are you all right?" He had watched the play of emotions across her face with concern. Ordinarily, he would have asked what was wrong, but he sensed the wall of privacy she had raised around herself and had the sensitivity not to try to breach it, at least not then.

"I'm fine," she assured him. "Do you think there might be any news about West?"

"If there was, we'd be told. I have another meeting scheduled with Gregory for this afternoon, but until then it would be best if I seemed to be going about a normal routine.''

"And if I stayed out of sight?'' she inquired with a smile.

"I'm afraid so. After all, you're supposed to be off the story due to illness.''

"Maybe I'll prowl around the embassy and see if I can pick up anything interesting,'' she suggested teasingly.

He laughed and leaned forward to lightly kiss her mouth. "How about just taking it easy instead?''

"I'm not sure I know how to do that,'' she admitted.

"Then it's time you learned. Take a bubble bath, do your nails, be frivolous.''

"That kind of talk could lead a girl astray,'' she said, though her eyes gleamed at the idea of a few hours of sybaritic indulgence. The novelty alone would make the experience worthwhile.

After another, longer kiss that sent a rush of warmth through her, he said, "That's the idea.''

"Oh, well, as long as we're clear on where we are.''

"Not yet, but we're getting there.''

With that he left her to soak in a hot tub that eased the tension from her body but did nothing at all to relieve her mind.

Chapter 13

Around noon, an aide popped his head into the living room where Judith was curled up, reading a Dick Francis mystery she had found, to inquire if she would join the ambassador and his children at lunch. She was happy to do so, if a little nervous, and the meal proved most enjoyable.

Jessie and Davey were both spirited but well behaved children. The little boy had the same blue eyes as his sister, but features that were more markedly Gavin's. There was an impish twinkle in his eye, and Judith did not doubt that he could be a handful. But he was also endearingly sweet, greeting her with a broad smile and appeared even more ready to accept her than did Jessie.

"That wasn't so bad, was it?" Gavin asked after the children had gone to play.

"It was fun." Sitting around the table with him and the children, she had felt almost part of a family, something she hadn't known for a long time.

"You don't do this sort of thing very often, do you?" he asked.

She shook her head. "My parents moved to Florida several years ago, and since then I haven't seen much of them."

He didn't ask why she was unable to make what was, by air at least, not a very long trip even when she was living in California. Instead, he said, "Do you have any brothers or sisters?"

She shook her head. "No, I was an only child. What about you?"

He laughed. "The opposite. Three sisters and two brothers. A grand total of fourteen nieces and nephews, with the fifteenth on the way."

"It must be incredible when you all get together," Judith said wistfully. "Do you ever do that?"

"Once a year, at my folks' place on Nantucket. It's a Christmas tradition."

It sounded wonderful. With very little effort, she could imagine herself taking part in such a gathering. While she might feel out of place at first, she had the feeling that his family could quickly make any stranger feel welcome.

The look in her eyes, carefully hidden in an instant, tugged at his heart. He was still thinking about it half an hour later when he returned to his office. At midafternoon, he was due at the palace. Between now and then, he would do his best to foster the impression that nothing unusual was going on.

He was dictating several letters to the formidable Miss Witherspoon when the phone rang. She picked it up briskly, identified herself, and listened for a moment before handing the receiver to him. "Mr. Berdot, sir."

"I hope I am not disturbing you, Mr. Ambassador," the security man said.

"Not at all. Is there something I can do for you?"

"His Highness would appreciate it if you could come over to the palace now, instead of later in the day."

That was a small enough request, which caused him to puzzle over the tenseness he heard in Berdot's voice. The man's concern went far beyond the routine courtesy appropriate to a change of plans.

"Of course," Gavin said. "I'll leave now."

Berdot rang off after murmuring his thanks. Gavin rose from behind his desk and reached for his jacket, only to find that Miss Witherspoon had beaten him to it. "Something wrong, sir?" she inquired.

"I'm not sure." She was, of course, fully aware of the threats against Althea, of West's disappearance, and of Judith's presence in the embassy. It would have been impossible to keep such facts from her, and Gavin knew that she could be trusted absolutely. He also valued her judgment. "Berdot is upset. My guess is something more has happened."

"I do hope not, sir." She said that sincerely but without any conviction that it was the case. After all her years in the diplomatic service Miss Witherspoon had expressed herself, convinced that any situation, no matter how bad, could always get worse.

"If I'm not back in a few hours," Gavin said, "I'd appreciate your telling Miss Fairchild where I've gone."

"You wish her kept informed, sir?"

"Completely."

Miss Witherspoon's gray eyebrows rose fractionally, but otherwise she had no comment. She didn't need to. He read in even that slight gesture both her acknowledgment and her approval.

Someday, he promised himself as he took the stairs to the back door, which would allow him an unobserved exit, he was going to shock Witherspoon. How, he had no idea, but there had to be a way. At least he wanted to think that there did.

He was shown into the palace through a rear entrance that he had used before on private visits to Gregory. A footman ushered him not into the royal office but into a small sitting room where Berdot waited. The security man was grim-faced as he asked Gavin to take a seat.

"His Highness will join us in a few moments," he said.

Gavin nodded but did not speak beyond a quiet greeting. He was certain now that there had been further developments, but he knew Berdot would not reveal them until the king was present.

The delay turned out to be very brief. Gregory came into the room, nodded to Gavin, and walked over to a chinoiserie liquor cabinet. "I need a drink," he said without preamble. "Will you gentlemen join me?"

Berdot declined; despite the royal invitation, etiquette did not quite accustom him to accepting such hospitality. But Gavin was more than inclined to accept. He had a feeling that such sustenance might prove useful in the next few minutes.

Gregory filled two crystal tumblers with ice and scotch, took a quick swallow of his, and said bluntly, "Althea is missing." He kept his head averted as he spoke. The husky rasp of his voice alone betrayed his intense emotion.

"The terrorists?" Gavin asked, though he already knew the answer.

Gregory nodded. "She was being driven to a party being given in her honor. The car was stopped by what appeared to be a stalled truck. When the bodyguards got out to investigate, they were gunned down."

"A very smooth operation," Berdot said, not admiringly but as a simple statement of fact. "These are not bunglers we are dealing with."

"Which makes their lack of demands all the more difficult to understand," Gregory said. "We've had a further communique, but it contains little information and no mention of what they want in order to return her safely."

"Are you sure they really have her?" Gavin asked.

This time it was Berdot who answered. "The Lady Althea's engagement ring was enclosed with the message."

There could be no question, then. Gavin sat down heavily, not even bothering to taste his drink. He knew that anything in his mouth at that moment would be like ashes. "They've made no demands?" he asked quietly.

"Unfortunately not," Berdot said. "If they had, we would have a better chance of figuring out who they are."

"Clearly," Gavin murmured, "they want something." He didn't have to go on. Both of the other men knew that whatever that something had to do with, it must involve the xanium.

Wearily, Gregory said, "I can hardly comprehend how a few rocks that have been here for millions of years can suddenly be of such consequence."

Berdot and Gavin exchanged a glance. They were both worried about the king, having never seen him so emotionally exhausted before. But that was hardly surprising, considering the terrible images that must be haunting him.

"Your Highness," Gavin began, "I'm sure you know that the United States will do anything possible to help."

Gregory took a deep breath and straightened his shoulders. "I appreciate that," he said, "and I have no intention of rejecting help from any quarter."

Gavin had an idea he knew what was coming. A moment later, he was proven correct when a footman opened the door to the sitting room, murmured a name, and stood aside to allow the new arrival entry.

Leonid Karischenekov, Ambassador from the Union of the Soviet Socialist Republics to the Kingdom of Gregoria, strode into the room. He carried a properly sympathetic expression on his round face and spoke with due solemnity as he addressed Gregory.

"Your Highness, may I express the outrage of my government at this atrocity and pledge our utmost assistance in achieving both the safe return of the Lady Althea and the punishment of the kidnappers."

"Thank you," Gregory said. He inclined his head in Gavin's direction. "I presume you two are acquainted."

Leonid's air of subdued compassion altered slightly. He unbent enough to give Gavin a smile that was downright friendly. "Ambassador Penderast and I have known each other for some time," he said.

Gavin raised his drink in a silent salute as he elaborated. "What Leonid means is that we have been occasional allies in the past, as unlikely as that may sound."

"I trust that means you are capable of cooperating in this instance," Gregory said.

"Cooperating?" Leonid accepted the king's gestured invitation to take a seat, all the while keeping his eyes on Gavin. "Is that what our American colleague has been suggesting?"

"You know it is," Gavin said bluntly. "Let's not beat around the bush, Leonid. There's no time for that." Turning to the king, he said, "The fact is, Your

Highness, my esteemed...colleague and I have already discussed the possibility of working together on this matter.''

His late-night phone call to Karischenekov had borne fruit. Though they would always be wary of each other, the two men had agreed that this was one time when they had better relax their suspicions long enough to at least give each other a chance. However, that was not quite the same thing as Leonid's actually saying he would work with the Americans.

"Between the two of us," Gavin went on, "we should be able to muster a great deal of help. Unless, of course, there's some reason for one of us not to want to do so."

"I do not like the sound of that," Leonid growled. "Are you suggesting that the U.S.S.R. would stoop to such disgraceful behavior?"

Gavin shrugged. "If the shoe fits..."

"How typical of the Americans! The moment something bad happens they try to blame the Russians. I will have you know that our goal is of the highest order—namely world peace—and our behavior matches it." He spoke matter-of-factly, without anger, a man going through a familiar ritual.

"Then you'll have no reason not to cooperate in finding the Lady Althea and her kidnappers," Gavin said smoothly.

Leonid had an appreciative gleam in his eye as he turned his attention to Gregory. "Your Highness, are you certain it is wise to trust the Americans in this matter? After all, it is well known that they can be quite ruthless in achieving their ends. Only look at their television, all the time people shooting one another. They are violent people who think justice comes from the barrel of a gun."

"Your Highness," Gavin interrupted, understanding well enough that the ritual had to run its course but anxious for it to do so, "surely we can be spared the polemics. What matters here is finding Althea."

"I must agree with Ambassador Penderast," Gregory said. "Whatever the philosophical differences between your two nations—and I realize they are great— I believe that you are sincere in your desire to secure the xanium for your own use. While Althea is endangered, I can make no promises that you will be successful."

"Then let us assist you," Leonid said, not quite ready to give in. "The Soviet Union has vast intelligence resources, which we will place at your disposal. You have only to say the word."

"I am saying it," Gregory reminded him. Before the Russian could break into too hearty a smile, he added, "And I am also requesting help from the Americans. It is my desire for you to work together to assist us in bringing a speedy end to this crisis."

"Give it up, Leonid," Gavin said, though he didn't really think it was necessary. Leonid had said what he felt he had to and was now prepared to accept the realities of the situation. "His Highness is right to ask both of us. That way, if either of us is involved, we'll be hard pressed to hide it. And between the two of us, we'll be able to cover the gamut of intelligence sources.''

"If I might point out," Berdot murmured discreetly, "the government of Gregoria is not without its own sources in that area."

"I did not mean to suggest that we are," Gregory assured him. "However, the more directions we can work in, the better chance we will have of success."

"Yes," Leonid said thoughtfully, "I see the point." He heaved himself up and held out a meaty hand rather ceremoniously to Gavin. "Very well, we will work together."

They shook on it under the watchful eye of the king, who managed a tired smile. "Thank you, gentlemen. Now, if you will excuse me, there are several appointments I must keep. It is essential to give every appearance of normality."

Gavin and Leonid both agreed that was best and took their leave. Outside the sitting room, with the door safely closed behind them, they glanced at each other warily.

"I suppose he's testing us," Leonid said quietly.

"That's certainly part of it," Gavin agreed as they started down the stairs. "If he's thinking of what I think he is—namely granting us both access to the xanium—he wants to see how well we can get along. Of course, he also genuinely needs our help."

"Ah, yes, a terrible thing. Such a lovely woman. We must get her back for him. Not, of course, that we have any idea where she could be," Leonid added hastily.

"No idea at all?" Gavin asked.

Leonid bristled. "Are you suggesting again that we are involved?"

"I'm saying—not suggesting—that you're as up-to-date as we are on who would want to stop the xanium deal. There are the Western Europeans...."

"Ah, yes, your allies," Leonid said gleefully. "Undoubtedly they are the number-one suspect."

"I don't think so," Gavin said. "Not that they wouldn't like to pressure Gregory into going along with them, but they wouldn't do it this way."

Leonid scoffed openly at that. "Men will do anything where enough power is involved."

"I thought you'd ruled out at least one possible culprit, namely yourselves."

"We have nothing to do with this," Leonid said firmly.

They had reached the back door of the palace and passed through it to the covered passageway beyond. From there it was only a brief walk beyond the gates. Together they strolled down the main street, well aware of what the sight of them in close conversation might arouse in certain quarters.

"What would you say to an aperitif?" Leonid asked as they passed a small cafe with a shaded awning out in front.

"Fine with me," Gavin agreed. "I could use a drink."

"Let's sit outside," Leonid suggested. "From here, we can be seen from the windows of both the English and French embassies. It will do them good to wonder what we are getting so cozy about."

Gavin was willing to fall in with that. He didn't mind tweaking the noses of the allied governments occasionally, particularly when they were doing their best to thwart U.S. intentions.

The two men took seats at a prominent table and settled back to enjoy the view as they chatted with apparent ease.

"Don't take this the wrong way, Leonid," Gavin said, "but you're absolutely certain that no one in Moscow is involved?"

The Russian took a sip of the Johnny Walker Red he had specified to the waiter and nodded. "Absolutely, but not because of that high moral business I was handing out to the king. Very simply, no one there is stupid enough to get involved in something like this."

Gavin took a sip of his vodka and tonic. "That's the same reason I'm convinced no one in Washington has a hand in it."

Leonid nodded. He popped a handful of salted peanuts in his mouth and chewed them thoughtfully. "Between ourselves we can admit that our respective governments have done some things that didn't bear too much close scrutiny, but this is beyond all. Only madmen would commit such a folly."

"There's always the Arabs."

"Why is it that at the slightest sign of terrorism, Americans mention Arabs?"

"Experience?"

"All right, it's conceivable they might pull something like this. But for what purpose?"

"I don't know," Gavin admitted. "Even presuming they could find out about the xanium, there doesn't seem to be anything they could hope to gain by involving themselves."

"That is indeed the problem," Leonid said, signaling the waiter to bring them both a refill. "Always in any such situation I ask myself 'what is the objective?' Here I cannot come up with an answer that makes any sense."

"I'm having the same problem," Gavin said. "If we're telling each other the truth and neither of our governments is involved, and if—as I believe—the Western Europeans are innocent, then the objective can't be securing use of the xanium, because that doesn't leave anyone who could use it."

"Precisely," Leonid said, pounding his open hand on the table so that the salt and pepper shakers, set out for more substantial meals, jumped into the air. "So if the objective isn't to get the xanium, then what is it? What else can be done with it?"

"It could be left where it is," Gavin ventured. "Except that doesn't make any sense either. To prevent its use, the terrorists would have to hold Althea forever. Eventually they'd be caught, or Gregory would abdicate, or something would happen to remove them as a factor."

"I agree," Leonid said. "We have ruled out securing the xanium and leaving it where it is. What's left?"

"Destroying it?" Gavin said slowly. "That's the only other possibility. As I'm sure you know, the total find of xanium amounts to no more than one hundred pounds, and if the ore is heated above two thousand degrees Farenheit, the isotope self-destructs."

"Goodbye, xanium," Leonid muttered. "Goodbye, nuclear defense."

"It would seem that way."

The two men stared at each other. Neither had to spell out the problem. Over the decades, the two super powers had tried numerous times to come to some sort of accord on nuclear weapons. There had been a few small successes, but generally the trend was dismal. More and bigger weapons were continually being built. And with them grew the nightmare fear that someday, if only by accident, they would be used. The only true hope of preventing that was to devise a way to render them harmless. Until that happened, humanity would be doomed to live on the edge of devastation.

The Russian broke the silence, his voice tight and hard. "But that would mean that we are dealing with a group of madmen who actually want a nuclear war to happen."

Gavin finished his drink. He swirled the melting ice cubes absently. His eyes were grave as they met Leonid's. "I can't believe that's the case, but maybe because I simply don't want to. We seem to have ruled out everything else. Yet," he added thoughtfully, "I keep thinking we've missed something."

"What?" Leonid demanded.

"I don't know. We've looked at it from every angle. There are only three things that can be done with the xanium: use it, not use it, or destroy it. What's left?"

"Don't ask me," Leonid grumbled. "I'm out of ideas. What could we have missed?"

"Nothing, so far as I can see." Gavin was silent for a moment before he said, "Maybe that's it. We're looking at it only from our perspective. We need to turn it around and see how it may look to others."

"And how," Leonid asked skeptically, "do you plan to do that, even presuming it would serve some useful purpose?"

"I'm not sure," Gavin admitted. "But we have to try. There's something here that we've overlooked, and I've got a very bad feeling it's going to blow up in our faces unless we figure it out fast."

Chapter 14

By late afternoon, Judith was bored, worried, and annoyed. She prowled around the sitting room, peered out the window, debated whether or not to take a nap, and wondered what on earth Gavin could be doing.

He had been gone much longer than she had expected. In addition to concern for his safety, she was plagued with thoughts that the crisis might be heating up and she was not, despite his implied promises, being kept informed.

Efforts to question his aide proved futile. Her inquiries were turned away politely but firmly. She had no further luck with his formidable secretary, who assured her that the moment the ambassador returned, she would be informed. Meanwhile, wouldn't a cup of tea be nice?

With the beginnings of a headache drumming behind her eyes, Judith decided what she really needed was some fresh air. She could hardly venture out on the streets and risk being seen, but she could enjoy the lovely garden behind the embassy, sheltered by a high stone wall that protected it from prying eyes.

She was seated there, watching a pair of finches dart after bread crumbs she had brought with her, when a pebble landed at her feet.

"Pssst."

She looked up, puzzled, but saw nothing and went back to her contemplation of the birds.

Another pebble landed, followed by an urgent whisper: "Judith, over here."

The golden head of Louis, Duke of Montfort, peered at her from around a bayberry bush. He gave her a devastating smile and beckoned to her. "Come over here."

Amused, she did as he said.

"I stopped by for a word with the cultural attache about a little benefit I'm arranging," he explained, "and saw you through a window. Considering that you're supposed to be recuperating from some unexplained malady, I thought perhaps I should be discreet about approaching you. Besides," he added with a mischievous gleam in his eye, "it's more fun this way."

"You're a natural intriguer," she told him teasingly. He was a welcome break from the anxious tedium of the day.

"My dear," he said, "what else makes life worth living? But tell me before I'm overwhelmed by curiosity, are you truly ill, or is this malady more of the heart?"

"I'm fine," Judith assured him, since she could hardly claim to be otherwise without arousing suspicion. As to the second part of his question, she preferred not to comment. "However, you could do me a favor and not mention seeing me here."

"Say no more," he assured her with a gallant bow. "My lips are sealed. Although I have to admit, the diminishing number of journalists panting over Cousin Gregory's wedding is bound to arouse some comment."

"What do you mean?" Judith inquired carefully.

"Only that this morning I absolutely had to get out of the city for a while and took a little jaunt in the hills. I saw that Mr. West in the company of some rather scruffy types who I'm sure could have nothing at all to do with the pending nuptials."

"You actually saw him?" Judith asked, hoping her excitement was properly concealed.

"Oh, yes. I remembered him quite well from the embassy party. Anyone that obnoxious is hard to forget."

"Louis," Judith said earnestly, "this could be really important. Do you know exactly where you were when you saw him?"

"More or less. Why?"

Judith hesitated. She had no idea how much Louis was or was not in his royal cousin's confidence. But nothing about the handsome Duke suggested that he was aware of the crisis at hand, and she hardly felt qualified to tell him. Yet neither could she ignore the importance of what he had seen.

"I'd like you to tell someone about it." She was thinking of Berdot, certain that the security man would regard such information as vital.

"Whatever you like, my dear," Louis said. He looked at her curiously, as though hoping she would explain further, but when she did not, he accepted that with his usual equanimity.

As it turned out, Berdot was not available when they phoned. She had to be content with having Louis tell what he had seen to an aide. That left her far from satisfied. She got the distinct impression that Louis simply wasn't taken very seriously. There was no telling when his information might be acted on or when she would finally hear of the results.

To do nothing except wait was becoming more and more difficult, if not impossible. Much as she wanted to keep her agreement with Gavin, she couldn't help but think that these new developments had changed everything.

"Now that we've gotten that business with West out of the way," Louis said when they had left the aide, "will you have dinner with me?"

"What's that?" Judith asked. Her mind was on other things and she hadn't really heard him.

The duke's handsome features contracted wryly. "My dear, you are devastating to my ego."

"I'm sorry," Judith said with a smile. "Actually, I'd love to have dinner with you, but I really should stay here."

"In case a certain someone returns?"

"Well, yes . . ." she admitted.

"Would you mind a terribly personal piece of advice?"

"I suppose not. . . ."

"Never let a man find you waiting for him. That's the shortest route to being taken for granted."

"Actually," she said, "there's a bit more involved here." Although she did think Louis had a point. Gavin had been away all day without a word to her. She had no idea of when he might be back or of what might be going on. The journalist in her was frustrated by that, and the woman—so vulnerable in love—was threatened.

She really was not comfortable sitting around waiting for him, yet neither could she forget everything that was happening and go off to dinner with Louis.

"I'll tell you what," she said. "Do you think we might take a drive up to where you saw West instead?"

He sighed mournfully. "That's really what you want to do?"

"If you wouldn't mind."

With a resigned shrug, he took her arm. "Never let it be said that chivalry is dead."

Judith smiled her thanks, which had the desired effect. He brightened up and entertained her with amusing stories about the court as they drove out of the capital city and headed south toward the coast.

"They were probably smugglers," he said when the talk finally turned again to West and the men he had been seen with. "Despite dear Gregory's best efforts, that continues to be a problem."

"What do they smuggle?" she asked.

"Gold, mainly." At her surprised look, he laughed. "Sounds very exotic, doesn't it? Much better than drugs or electronics, which have absolutely no glamour. But the fact is, this part of the world has been a crossroads for gold smuggling for centuries."

"I wasn't aware that Gregoria had any gold."

"We don't, unless you count the rather nice stack of it in the royal treasury. No, we're simply a way station for gold from the Middle East, India, even Russia and the Orient. The smuggling routes reach through Gregoria into all parts of Western Europe. A great deal of the gold that flows through here ends up under the mattresses of proper Frenchmen and buried in the backyards of stalwart Britons."

"That's fascinating," Judith said. "I might consider doing a story on it when this is all over."

"I wouldn't advise it. The...gentlemen...involved in the gold trade tend to be very close-mouthed. They don't take kindly to people asking questions, not even lovely ladies."

Judith didn't say so, but that particular piece of information did not disturb her. She had dealt with plenty of people who didn't want to answer questions and had learned how to look out for herself in the process.

They were following a winding road that skirted the coastline, giving them a distant view of misty waters. Near the horizon, clouds hung low and dark, suggesting that a storm might be brewing, but overhead the sky was clear.

"It's so lovely here," Judith said as she tilted her head back and breathed deeply of the air scented with wild rosemary and thyme. "I'd hate to see the essential character of this place ever change."

Louis cast her a quick look from behind the wheel of the powerful Maserati that was eating up the miles. "A great many of us feel that way."

"Yet I suppose nothing can ever really stay the same."

"Gregoria has, for a very long time. While the rest of the world has gone its mad way, we've remained peaceful, serene, safe."

"Yet you can't cut yourself off from the rest of the world," she countered. "We're all being drawn closer and closer together through communication and travel. No one can remain apart."

"It would be very difficult," he acknowledged. "So long as disruptive influences exist, they can always find some way to get past even the most stringent security."

The mention of security brought Judith back to thinking about the threats against Althea. Again she wondered how much Louis knew. Certainly if he and Gregory were at all close, his cousin would have confided in him. But she had the sense that the men were no more than polite acquaintances, and that only by virtue of their family relationship.

"I suppose," she ventured, "you're looking forward to the wedding."

Louis shrugged. "There is a great deal of pressure on Gregory to produce an heir."

"I got the impression that isn't really why he's marrying."

"No," the duke agreed with a short laugh, "he's actually in love with Althea. Very amusing, given his . . . what do you call it . . . track record?"

"Yes, he was quite a playboy, wasn't he?"

Louis nodded. "For years, we'd all just about decided he would never marry."

And therefore never produce an heir, which brought up an interesting question. "What's the line of succession here? Would you become king if Gregory died childless?"

"What a mind you have," Louis said with a quick smile as he maneuvered the powerful car. "Gregory is not only several years younger than I, but also impeccably healthy. There was never any reason to think of him dying."

"Except that he did take part in a lot of dangerous sports," Judith said, almost to herself. "Car racing, polo, that sort of thing. He might have had an accident."

"Not with his luck," Louis said flatly. "He leads a charmed life." With a laugh that sounded surpris-

ingly humorless, he added, "Or at least he did up until now."

That brought Judith up short. Carefully, she asked,
"What do you mean?"

Louis no longer looked quite the genial bon vivant
she was used to seeing. Instead his mouth was set in a
hard line and his eyes were narrowed. "Only that no
one can expect to lead such a charmed life as Gregory
has without ultimately having to pay a price."

"I wouldn't say his life has been exactly charmed.
After all, he does have enormous responsibilities as
king."

"Don't imagine that he takes them seriously. Gregoria is no more than another plaything to him, something to amuse himself with without thought of the
consequence."

"I hadn't realized," Judith said slowly, "how much
you dislike him."

Instead of answering directly, Louis said, "Did you
know that Gregory and I are the sons of twin
brothers? Had my father been born a few minutes
sooner, I would be king today."

"And you would like to be, wouldn't you?"

"It is not a question of liking," he said stiffly. "It
is a matter of duty. Gregoria must be saved from my
cousin's careless plans."

"You mean to bring about change?"

"Exactly. He has no conception of what that will
mean . . . of all we will lose. We will become like every
place else, and it will be only a matter of time before

the monarchy is no more than a figurehead, as in Britain.''

The car was turning west toward the foothills of the Thessaly mountains. Above them the sky was turning red as the sun descended.

"I thought," Judith said, "that you had seen West near the coast."

"That's what I said."

"But is it true?"

"No, but if and when that dolt of an aide sees fit to relay the information, it will keep Berdot and his minions looking in the wrong direction."

Judith's hands were clasped tightly in her lap. Despite the warmth of the spring evening, she felt suddenly cold. "Stop the car. I'd like to get out now."

"And do what?" he challenged. "Walk back? No, my dear, I'm afraid that's quite out of the question." To emphasize his point, he speeded up. The narrow road whizzed by at upwards of seventy miles an hour. To attempt to jump out of the car would be suicide.

"You can't get away with this," Judith said desperately.

Louis laughed; he was actually enjoying himself. "Such a cliche. I expected better from you."

"Sorry," she muttered, forcing herself to relax somewhat. There was no possibility of getting away from Louis at the moment, but eventually he would have to stop the car. They must be going somewhere, and when they got there she would find some way to escape. Or at least she hoped she would.

"Where are we going?" she asked, thinking that the more she could get him to talk, the better chance she had of picking up information that might prove useful.

"Somewhere safe."

"We're getting close to the mountains. Is that where we're going?"

"You ask too many questions," he snarled. "Be quiet."

Judith ignored the order. Though she didn't doubt now that Louis could be dangerous, she was willing to push him at least a little further. "Why did you bring me along? I can't be of any use to you."

"Don't be so sure of that."

"If you're thinking that my network will pay a ransom or give you air time, you're wrong."

"I told you to be quiet," Louis said. "My patience is running out."

"It's my business to ask questions."

His hands tightened on the steering wheel until the knuckles turned white. "You are here not as a reporter but as a woman."

That threw her; she had no idea why he should make such a distinction, but she definitely didn't like the sound of it. "What do you mean?"

"It's quite simple." So much so, his tone suggested, that even she should be able to see it. "You and Ambassador Penderast have become lovers. He is known to be a very discriminating man, not lightly given to such amours. Chances are then that he genuinely cares for you and will do what he must to protect you."

"You're going to use me to blackmail him?" Judith asked incredulously.

"To assure his cooperation," Louis corrected. "I want no problems from the Americans, now or later. I'm sure to save you, he will persuade his government to publicly recognize me as ruler of Gregoria. Once they are committed to me, they will not be able to back out. Now, unless you want me to gag you, you will be quiet."

She took that threat seriously and lapsed into silence, her mind working feverishly.

A multitude of questions were on the tip of her tongue, but she did not voice them. She sensed that the further they drove, the tenser Louis became, and she did not want to test his fragile patience any more.

At length they turned onto a narrow dirt road that might be more correctly described as a goat path. Louis pulled the car behind a concealing outcropping of rock and gestured at her to get out.

"If you have any idea of running away," he said, "I hope this will discourage you." From the inside pocket of his jacket, he drew a small but lethal-looking pistol. Gesturing with the gun, he said, "We go that way. You first."

Judith obeyed him, mainly because she could see no alternative. While she wasn't absolutely certain that he would shoot her, finding out for sure didn't seem like a good idea. Resignedly, she began to climb up the path, which became steadily steeper and rougher.

Although she was in good shape, her breath slowly became labored, and she stumbled once or twice. When it happened again, Louis cursed and gave her a rough push. "Hurry up. We don't have all day."

With an effort, she regained her balance and went on. They were climbing steadily higher and were well into the mountains. The air was cooler, and her thin khaki jacket gave her little protection. She shivered and would have put her hands in her pockets, except that she needed them to grab hold of the small, scrubby bushes that she used to pull herself along.

They rounded a bend and confronted a large mountain goat, which stared at them majestically before it ambled off. Far below Judith could see the winding course of the river that ran past the capital. There were a scattering of villages and, closer by, a handful of huts, but all were too far away to consider as any source of help.

"Stop here," Louis said at last, to her great relief. She straightened, breathing deeply and slowly, as she looked around. There was nothing in sight; the goat path ended where they stood, and above it was a sheer rock face that could be climbed only with rope and grappling hooks. She was hoping that wasn't what Louis had in mind when he suddenly whistled three times in a short but unmistakable signal.

A young man in pseudo-military dress appeared from behind a large thorn bush. He held an automatic rifle in his hands and looked ready to use it, until he recognized Louis and saluted instead.

The man stood aside as Louis took Judith's arm and pulled her around to the other side of the bush. She gasped when she saw that it concealed the entrance to a cave. But she had barely a moment to think about that before she was pushed forward into darkness.

Chapter 15

Gavin stood with his hands on his hips, glaring in disbelief at his aide. "How the hell could she have left here without anyone stopping her?"

"We had no instructions to detain her, sir. Besides, she was leaving with the Duke of Montfort. If we had attempted to stop him, we would have caused a diplomatic incident. At least," he added, brightening, "we know where she went."

"For a drive along the coast road, on some wild goose chase after West," Gavin said with disgust.

"The duke did say he saw him there."

"What about it, Berdot?" Gavin demanded. He had summoned the security man to the embassy as soon as he learned of Judith's absence. Normally he would not have done so, knowing that the older man already had more than enough to cope with. But the situation worried him deeply, and he wasn't about to stand on niceties. "Do you think there's anything to what the duke claimed to see?" he demanded.

Berdot shrugged. Discreetly, he said, "It is hard to say, sir."

"But you must have some idea. Is Louis considered reliable?"

"We have no reason to believe that he is not."

"That doesn't answer my question," Gavin said tautly. "I'm asking whether or not he can be trusted."

Berdot glanced at the aide meaningfully, then back to Gavin, who took the hint. "That's all," he told the younger man. "If I need you again, I'll ring."

When they were alone, he turned to Berdot and said, "Enough pussyfooting. Out with it."

The security man spread his hands as though asking for understanding. "It is a very difficult situation. You are not Gregorian, and even if you were, I would hesitate to speak too frankly on such a delicate matter."

"Then perhaps I should ask the king instead."

Berdot grimaced and shook his head. "His Highness already has more than enough to concern him." He paused for a moment, then went on abruptly. "All right, the fact of the matter is that there are those of us who do not believe the duke is what he seems. He appears on the surface to be loyal to the king, completely accepting of his own subordinate position. Yet he is also a man of great pride who on more than one occasion has shown himself to possess a dangerous temper. And he is believed to be unalterably opposed to the policy of modernization that His Highness has brought to the country."

"Is that a long way of saying you think he may be a traitor?"

"I would not put it quite so harshly...."

Gavin slammed his fist down on a nearby table and demanded, "Damn it, is he a threat or isn't he?"

"He...may be."

"And Judith's with him."

This last part was uttered so softly that Berdot barely caught it. But there was no mistaking the anguish that crossed Gavin's face. Gently Berdot said, "There is no reason to believe that Miss Fairchild is in any danger."

"I can think of at least one," Gavin muttered. An idea was forming in his mind, so outrageous that he could hardly credit it, yet it would not go away. "We *were* looking at it in the wrong way," he said.

"I beg your pardon, sir," a puzzled Berdot said.

"Leonid and I, we were only thinking of it from our own perspective. What we wanted to gain. But we're not behind all this. There's another motive, apart from the xanium."

Berdot frowned. "I don't think I'm following you."

"Oh, the xanium is important, all right, but it's not the primary objective. That's why we couldn't make it add up." Lost in his train of thought, Gavin barely noticed Berdot's baffled look as he paced up and down.

After several minutes of this, the security man said, "Mr. Ambassador, I really must get back to the palace."

"Yes, of course…go ahead. But I'll come with you. I've got to talk with the king."

He was actually smiling, much to Berdot's amazement, but then he had never pretended to understand Americans.

Neither had Gregory, and he for one had no intention of trying, not after Gavin had spelled out his theory for him. "That's absolutely absurd," the king said firmly. "I realize you are concerned about Miss Fairchild, but to think for a moment that Louis could have anything to do with this…"

"He's the explanation behind the rumors we've been hearing," Gavin insisted, ignoring the king's anger, "about an attempt underway to overthrow your government. Overthrow it and replace it with what? The Gregorians are hardly going to accept some sort of revolutionary council or anything of that ilk. But they would go along with the orderly succession of the monarchy." Looking at Gregory directly, he said, "The Duke of Montfort is your heir, isn't he?"

"At the moment," the king admitted reluctantly, "until I have a son."

"And to do that, you have to marry. Except that your fiancée is missing."

"And from that you conclude Louis is responsible? It makes no sense. If something happened to Al-

thea—'' a dark look passed across his face ''—I would
be expected to marry someone else.''

''Would you?''

''I . . . don't know.''

Gavin thought it highly unlikely that any alternative marriage would occur within the near future. He
knew in his own case how many years had had to pass
before he could love any woman besides Carrie. But
be that as it may, he had other concerns.

''Besides, I'm not sure Althea is the ultimate target. My guess is she's merely the bait.''

Both Gavin and Berdot were surprised by the startled look that passed over the king's features. But
when he said nothing, Gavin felt compelled to ask,
''Have you heard from the kidnappers again?''

To the security man's surprise, the king nodded. ''A
few minutes ago. They are asking for a private meeting with me.''

''Your Highness,'' Berdot blurted, ''I strongly recommend against that.''

''So do I,'' Gavin added. ''It ties in perfectly with
what I suspect. Louis isn't out to kill Althea; it's you
he's after.''

''It's monstrous to even suggest that my cousin
could contemplate such a crime,'' Gregory said. ''You
aren't talking simply about murder but about regi-
cide.''

''I'm talking about an ambitious man seeing a last
chance to gain what he thinks ought to be his. Once
you marry, odds are you'll have an heir quickly and
Louis will be out of luck, so it has to be now or never.''

"I can't believe it . . ." Gregory insisted.

"If you go to meet with the kidnappers, you'll be going to your own death."

"But if I do not, Althea . . ." His voice broke. He turned away to hide his emotion from the two other men.

Gavin gave him a moment, then put a hand on his shoulder and said quietly, "There's another way."

The darkness of the cave had given way gradually to a shadowy light in which Judith could perceive the shapes of several more men with guns who were crouched around a small fire, drinking coffee and talking among themselves. Their leader, a short, squat man with piercing eyes, had risen quickly when Louis entered. The two of them were off to one side in apparently intense discussion.

Judith had been told to sit on a rock some little distance from the fire and not move if she valued her life. Since she certainly did, she was trying to obey, but fear and curiosity were getting the better of her. She understood instinctively that the more she could learn about her surroundings, the better chance she would have of getting away. Though with so many armed men, the possibility of escape seemed remote.

Still she refused to give up hope and was just beginning to get her bearings in the cave when a low moan distracted her. Cautiously, she peered into the darkness beyond the fire, making out at last the shapes of two bodies whose unnatural postures made it clear they were not sleeping.

Two? She knew that West might well be there, but who was the other person, and were they badly hurt?

Glancing at the guards, she saw that they were still busy with their coffee and their talk. Louis was similarly occupied. She hesitated a moment, then slowly slid off the rock and crawled in the direction of the bodies.

She made out West first, and breathed a sigh of relief when she discovered that though he was bound and gagged, he was still conscious. His eyes widened in surprise at the sight of her, and she had to be grateful for the dirty kerchief that kept him from blurting out her presence. Quickly she passed on to discover the identity of the other captive.

Althea! A gasp broke from Judith, which she quickly stifled. The young woman lay on her side, her golden hair spread out in the dirt. There was a bruise on her cheek, and her breathing was shallow. Unlike West, she was deeply unconscious.

Oh, my God... Judith didn't say the words out loud—caution was too alive in her now to allow for that—but she did speak them in her mind in a silent, fervent prayer.

It was even worse than she had thought. If they had taken Althea, they must be deadly serious about getting whatever it was they wanted from Gregory. And how could he refuse to give it to them when by doing so he could be condemning to death the woman he loved?

A hard hand on her shoulder made her cry out. She turned to find Louis glaring down at her. "I told you to stay where you were."

"She's hurt," Judith shot back. Frightened though she was, she could not hide her loathing for this man. He was weak and treacherous, everything that she despised. "You can't leave her like this. She could die."

A queer smile twisted his lips. "Wouldn't that be a shame?"

A tremor of dread ran through her. She forced it down and said, "At least untie her and let me take care of her."

Louis shrugged. "Why not. It will keep you out of trouble." He drew a knife from the leather strap concealed up his sleeve and cut Althea's bonds. Judith quickly undid the gag around her mouth. Before she had finished, West was thrashing about wildly, trying to get both her and the duke's attention.

"What about him?" she asked, correctly interpreting the other man's frantic movements.

Louis shook his head. "He stays as he is, and if you make one false move, you'll join him."

Judith took the warning seriously. She ignored West, much to his chagrin, and concentrated on Althea.

Near where she lay, there was a small underground stream. Judith moistened her handkerchief and used it to gently wash the young woman's face. She kept this up for perhaps fifteen minutes before she was rewarded by a soft moan and the fluttering of eyelashes.

Slowly Althea opened her eyes and gazed up at her. She was clearly bewildered, not understanding what had happened to her or where she was.

"It's all right," Judith murmured. "You're safe for the moment." That much she believed, but she wasn't betting on their having very long life expectancies unless circumstances changed radically.

"The guards..." Althea murmured as she struggled to sit up. "With me... in the car..."

"I don't know what happened to them," Judith said, though she doubted it was anything good. "We're in a cave somewhere in the Thessaly mountains. My guess is it's one of those old hermit caves I heard about. Anyway, Louis is behind all this. He seems to have some idea he's going to save Gregoria."

"He hates Gregory," Althea whispered. She was very pale, and the bruise on her cheek stood out in stark contrast to the whiteness of her skin. But she was rapidly regaining control of herself, for which Judith was grateful. "I've always suspected it," she went on, "though I knew Gregory would never believe it."

"He'll have to now," Judith said grimly, even as she wondered what else he would have to do. A terrible suspicion was forming in her mind. She glanced back over her shoulder where Louis was sitting with the other men. "Althea, Louis wants to be king, doesn't he?"

At the younger woman's nod, she added, "And there's only one way he can do that."

What little color had returned to Althea's cheek faded, but she held on to her composure admirably. "We must get away from here."

But how? Neither woman had to voice the question. Louis and the guards were between them and the entrance to the cave. They had no weapons and no hope of getting them by surprise, at least not then.

"We'll have to wait," Judith said, "and pray that they get careless."

Meanwhile, there was West to think of. Lacking though she was in sympathy for him, she didn't think he should remain trussed up like a suckling pig awaiting the fire.

With great effort, she managed to assume a properly humbled expression and made her way back to Louis. "Excuse me," she said deferentially.

He looked up, took in her subdued air, and smiled. "What is it?"

"I was just wondering if you might reconsider about West. He is extremely uncomfortable."

"That does not concern me."

"I see . . . Well, if you really think he's a threat to you . . ."

Pride could hardly allow Louis to admit that. Stiffly, he said, "Very well, I will untie him, but if you have any notions about trying to escape, please keep in mind that your deaths would not weigh heavily on my conscience."

Since she very much doubted that he had any such thing, Judith could well believe him. West sat up gingerly after Louis had unfastened his bonds. There was real fear in his eyes as he watched the duke return to his men. She couldn't really blame him for being afraid but hoped he would be able to get himself under control if he was going to be of any help.

That didn't seem likely as West moaned, "Oh, God, I can't believe this is happening. It's a nightmare."

"Really?" she said. "I would have thought you'd be all excited about being on the inside of such an incredible story."

"What good will that do me," he demanded petulantly, "if we all wind up dead?"

"Oh, come on," she said with far more confidence than she was feeling. "That's not going to happen. They'll just hold us until they get what they want."

West continued to look doubtful, but at least it occurred to him to wonder about someone other than himself. "What about her?" he asked, cocking his head in Althea's direction.

"I guess we'll just have to wait and see," Judith said, as though it didn't really matter to her one way or another.

When she had West sufficiently quieted down, she went back to Althea and said, "I don't think we can count on him for much help."

"It's just as well. I prefer to count on ourselves."

That attitude reassured Judith, who agreed with it completely. But she was still stymied as to what to do. "Any ideas?"

"Several," Althea said with a wry smile, "but I'm afraid they're all a little unrealistic."

"I know what you mean." Judith was also entertaining fantasies about what she would like to do to the renegade duke, none of them particularly pleasant. "The problem as I see it is that they're between us and the entrance."

"And they've got the guns," Althea pointed out.

"There is that...."

"Judith...don't think in terms of getting us all out of here. Think about yourself."

Her eyes met those of the younger woman's, reading in them a knowledge she did not want to see. "Don't be silly," she said briskly. "We'll all get away."

"That's not very likely."

"Let me tell you something. I've been in tight spots before, and I know all about beating the odds. Besides, we've got hours yet. They're waiting for something, and whatever it is, it can't happen before dawn."

"They're waiting for Gregory," Althea said, her voice low and anguished. "Nothing else makes any sense. They're using me as bait to lure him here."

Judith agreed with her, but she wasn't about to say so. "Maybe, maybe not. There's no point in jumping to any conclusions. What we need to do is divert their attention so they won't be watching us as closely as they should."

"I saw a movie once," Althea said slowly, "where some convicts lit a fire in a truck that was transporting them, and when the guards tried to put it out they got away."

"That's the ticket," Judith exclaimed. Her first flush of enthusiasm faded as she added, "Only there doesn't seem to be anything to burn around here, except the wood they're using."

"We could always try to seduce them," Althea suggested, "except that I don't think I have a strong enough stomach for that."

"Neither do I," Judith admitted. Why did daredevil escapes look so easy in the movies and turn out to be so tough in real life? For that matter, where was the cavalry when you really needed them?

They were sitting close together in the dim shadows cast by the fire, trying vainly to come up with some sort of plan, when West slumped down beside them. "I tried talking to the duke. He isn't interested in doing an interview."

"Very short-sighted of him," Judith murmured. "You could have made him a star."

West cast her a sharp look, clearly suspecting that she was making fun of him. Fortunately, his ego was still strong enough for him to dismiss the possibility. "Yeah, that's what I told him, but he didn't see the benefits. At least not yet." More cheerfully he added, "Maybe he'll change his mind."

"Keep working on him," Judith advised. "He won't be able to withstand your charm."

"I am pretty good at convincing people," West admitted modestly. He turned to Althea. "How about you? When this is all over, I could get you on television—that is, if you're still . . . uh . . ."

Judith rolled her eyes and went back to thinking about escape, as much to get away from West as the duke.

She was still pondering the dilemma, without any success, when a low, persistent sound from somewhere behind her finally penetrated her consciousness. She turned absently, looking over her shoulder into the deepest recesses of the cave.

Nothing. It must have been her imagination. With a sigh she told herself to concentrate on the problem at hand. For a few minutes that worked, until the sound came again.

This time she was sure she had heard it, the faintest suggestion of breathing from behind her. Giant bats? Cave creatures? Or . . .

"I'm going to take a look farther back," she whispered to Althea. "If anyone notices I'm gone, tell them I'm answering a call of nature."

Gathering her courage around her, she moved slowly into the stygian darkness. Even a few additional feet from the camp fire, she could barely make out her hand in front of her face. Every instinct she possessed told her to turn back, but she could not. The breathing she had heard was more distinct and coming from nearby.

Telling herself that she had nothing to lose, she kept going, feeling her way along the damp cave wall. Until her fingers encountered something warm and hard. They jerked back, and reflexively she opened her mouth to scream. . . .

Only to stop abruptly when she found herself looking straight into the kindly face of Sebastian, wagon driver, provider of lifts to damsels in distress, raconteur of Gregorian history, and apparently a man given to turning up in the unlikeliest places at the most opportune times.

Chapter 16

"How..." Judith murmured, "how did you get in here?"

"The usual way," Sebastian said. His deep voice rumbled softly in the darkness. "Let us say that I prefer back entrances."

"Then there is one." Hope flowed through her. There might, after all, be a way to escape.

"Indeed," her companion confirmed. "This cave runs deep into the mountain and emerges on the other side near a field. Having two ways in and out has made it very useful."

Judith was beginning to understand. The gold smugglers who Louis himself had said were active throughout Gregoria would have needed some place to store their precious bullion bars safe from prying eyes. And they would value a hiding place in which they could not be trapped.

"Does the duke know?" she asked urgently.

"He has no idea…about a great many things. I have been watching and listening. What he intends is very bad."

"Yes, I'm afraid it is," Judith said, glad that she didn't have to explain the situation to him. "We have to get the Lady Althea away from here."

Sebastian nodded but cautioned, "We must wait until they are less alert. I know men like this; if they are threatened, they will panic. You have an expression in America—shoot first and ask questions later. That is what will happen here, except that there will be no questions."

"Do you really think they will become less vigilant?"

"There is a risk they will not," Sebastian admitted. "But they are very confident against two women and the cowardly Mr. West. That can breed carelessness."

There were few things Judith wanted to do less than return to her place in the cave and wait to see if Sebastian's guess was right. But she could see no alternative. To attempt to stage an escape while Louis and the other men were alert would be suicide. There was no choice except to wait.

If she thought her patience had been tried in the past, she quickly learned how sorely strained it could become. In addition to the fear that no opportunity to get away would arise, she also had to battle the temptation to tell Althea about Sebastian and the second

entrance to the cave. If they could only have gotten a
moment alone together, she would have done so. But
West clung to their sides, jumping at his own shadow
and emitting self-pitying groans that quickly put both
their tempers on edge.

"I wish he would be quiet," Althea whispered
wearily. "He makes it very hard to think."

Judith didn't have to ask what she was thinking
about. Althea was faced with a nightmare situation,
knowing that she was being used to lure the man she
loved quite possibly to his death. She had to be desperately trying to come up with some way to avoid
that. Judith could only pray that she didn't do anything precipitous.

The hours passed slowly. Louis and his men ate, but
no food was offered to their captives. A bottle of wine
was passed around, followed by another. Judith
perked up when she saw that and exchanged an en-
couraging glance with Althea. But the men's capacity
for alcohol was apparently great, and they showed no
sign of being affected by what they drank.

They did, however, become more relaxed and gar-
rulous, boasting among themselves of their bravery
and their exploits, both military and amatory. Apparently they regarded themselves as heroes, a belief
Louis encouraged even as he held himself aloof from
the discussion.

Judith couldn't help but notice that he did not share
his men's wine but drank instead from a silver flask of
his own. He took short, quick swallows and forgot
himself enough to wipe his mouth with the back of his

hand. Such a lapse in appearances in a man who counted on them so heavily told her that he was getting very nervous.

Several times she caught him fingering the knife he carried and glancing in the direction of his prisoners, particularly at Althea, who had slumped into an exhausted silence that did not bode well for her state of mind. Without understanding precisely how she knew, Judith came to the conclusion that they could not afford to wait much longer.

Tempted though she was to creep back into the cave and tell Sebastian what she feared, she remained where she was. This time she was rewarded for her patience. Louis continued to drink from the silver flask, which was replenished on his order from a large bottle of fine old brandy. The men continued to drink their wine. Gradually the talk petered away.

"I need some rest," Louis announced rather grandly as he gestured to one of the men to spread out a blanket for him near the fire. "I want to be fresh for my royal cousin tomorrow." He laughed sharply at that. "The rest of you stay on guard."

No one dissented—they were hardly the sort to do so—but Judith privately doubted that was an order that would be obeyed. With their leader setting the example, the men would see no reason to remain awake.

After Louis had wrapped himself in his blanket, turned his back on the others, and begun to snore, his men wasted no time following suit. One by one, they stretched out, got as comfortable as they could on the hard ground, and drifted off.

Judith waited for perhaps half an hour before she gently nudged Althea. "Look," she whispered, indicating the sleeping men.

Althea saw what she was supposed to but had no way of interpreting its importance. "They are still between us and the cave entrance," she said morosely.

Judith shook her head. Afraid to say too much and risk waking one of the men, she nodded her head toward the back of the cave. It took Althea a moment to realize what she was telling her. When she did, her eyes opened wide in question. Judith nodded, then looked at West, who had at last fallen silent and lay staring hopelessly off into space.

Both women stifled a sigh. It was tempting to think of leaving him behind; in his preoccupation with his own safety he wouldn't notice that they were gone. But they could not bring themselves to let him face Louis's retribution by himself.

Judith leaned over and tugged at his sleeve. It took him a moment to react, and when he did he looked at her impatiently, as though annoyed at having his morose reverie interrupted.

"Follow us," she whispered, then immediately withdrew, leaving him no time to ask questions or argue.

Swiftly, she and Althea moved farther into the cave. After a moment they could hear West behind them, stumbling and making more noise than he should as he hurried to catch up.

"What's going on?" he demanded. "We could get in trouble for this."

"For heaven's sake," Judith hissed, "we're already in trouble. If you'll just be quiet, maybe we can get out of it."

Instead of following her suggestion, West protested. "I can hardly see a foot in front of myself. We could fall in a hole or who knows what."

"Mr. West," Althea said, "if you do not stop talking instantly, I will tell the king that you deliberately endangered my safety. You will then have a very interesting story to tell about what it's like inside a Gregorian prison."

West opened his mouth to reply, thought better of it, and blessed silence reigned. Through it, Judith strained to hear any sound of pursuit. When there was none, she took a deep breath of relief, then turned her attention to finding Sebastian.

He was waiting near a turn in the tunnel that led back through the cave. Upon catching sight of him, West almost forgot his newly minted vow of silence, but remembered just in time to hold his tongue. Sebastian himself did not make a sound; he merely raised his hand and urged them on in the right direction.

They followed him quickly, mindful that at any moment Louis or one of his men might wake and find them gone. But before that could happen, a faint glimmer of light shone from deep in the cave. They hurried toward it, relishing the fresh breeze that heralded their escape.

Emerging from the cave, they found themselves above a field bathed in moonlight. Steep, rock-strewn ground led down toward it. They had just begun the descent when a shot behind them warned that time had run out.

"Get down!" Sebastian ordered, pushing the women behind an outcropping of rock an instant before bullets whizzed past.

West tumbled in after them, cursing mightily. "I knew this wouldn't work! We should have stayed where we were, worked something out with the duke. He's not a barbarian, for God's sake! We could have made a deal."

"Using what?" Judith demanded, making no effort to hide her disgust. "A promise that we'd look the other way when he murdered Gregory and Althea?"

"That's not what he—"

"You know it is! Not even you can think otherwise. Now, shut up and let the rest of us figure out what to do!"

So taken aback was he by her harsh but accurate indictment that he did as she said. Sebastian stuck his head up above the rocks for an instant, drawing more fire, and returned with a gloomy assessment.

"There are four of them, including the duke. The rest must have gone out the front entrance on the chance that we had somehow gotten past them. At least we've managed to divide their force, but they still have us outgunned."

Considering that among them they had only a pistol of ancient vintage that Sebastian pulled from the pocket of his jacket, this was undoubtedly the case. Pinned down behind the rocks, they could be picked off at Louis's leisure.

Except that he apparently wasn't in the mood for such sport. "Judith," he called suddenly, "I want to talk with you."

She looked at Althea and Sebastian, shrugged, and called back, "Go ahead."

"Come out first. I guarantee your safety."

"Please, Louis, I'm in no mood to laugh."

"This is serious," he complained, clearly offended by her dismissive tone.

"I know! That's why I'm not coming out."

"You'll have to eventually. You know that."

"I can wait." Let him chew on that, she thought grimly. With any luck, he would think they were expecting rescuers and wanted to keep him in place until they arrived.

That suspicion must have occurred to the duke, for he shouted back, "I'm running out of patience. You don't want to turn this into a bloodbath, do you?"

"I thought that was what you had in mind all along."

Silence for several moments as he digested how much she had figured out. With an almost cloying tone of reassurance, he said, "There's no need to be melodramatic. We're all civilized people. We'll discuss this and work something out."

"I told you," West exclaimed. "You can sit here till hell freezes over if you want, but I'm doing what the man says." Before they could make any move to stop him, he jumped up, his hands in the air, and shouted, "It's West, your...uh...dukeship. I'm coming out. You won't have any trouble with me."

In his haste, he stumbled and fell twice before he was able to reach the duke's position above the rock outcropping. Once there he vanished from sight, pulled down by several of Louis's men. The three left behind the rocks heard a brief exclamation that might have been from West, then nothing more.

Until Louis called down to them, "You have three minutes to surrender. After that, I will not be responsible for what happens."

"Typical," Judith muttered. In her travels around the world, often to "hot spots," she had noticed that those most inclined to violence took great pains to disassociate themselves from all responsibility before they wreaked their havoc. Generally—and, she felt, obscenely—they blamed their victims.

Althea put a hand on her arm and said urgently, "You must not stay here. He will kill us all if you do."

"Are you suggesting we give up, my lady?" Sebastian asked.

She hesitated a moment, then nodded. "I am. At least that way you have a chance of surviving."

"And what about you?" Judith asked.

"I...cannot. He will use me to hurt Gregory."

"He'll try, but he won't necessarily succeed."

"That is not a risk I can take."

"Please," Judith entreated, "you can't throw away your own life. Gregory wouldn't want that."

"I know," Althea said with a wan smile. "But it is he I must think of. I am praying that unless Louis can actually produce me, alive and well, Gregory will not come close enough to them to be harmed. That is the only hope I have."

"One minute," Louis shouted.

"There is still a chance, my lady," Sebastian insisted, pleading with her.

"Is there?" She pointed across the field, drawing their attention for the first time to the thin cloud of dust rising from a single vehicle making its way toward them. By the moonlight, they could see only one man in it, on whose shoulders glinted the epaulets of a Royal Hussar's uniform.

"Time's up," Louis called. "Surrender now or we'll fire."

"Go quickly!" Althea urged. "I do not want your deaths on my conscience."

"Wait," Judith said. She looked more closely at the approaching vehicle and her heart leaped into her throat. "It's not . . ."

A spray of automatic weapon fire from the ledge above them cut off her words. "That's my final warning," Louis yelled. She did not believe that she imagined the keen edge of desperation in his voice. His great plan was about to reach its climax, so he thought, and the key ingredient for its success still eluded him. Without Althea, he could not lure Gregory to his death.

"We can hold out a few more minutes," Judith insisted. "He'll have to move his men around to the other side of the ledge to get a clear shot at us."

"But Gregory—" Althea said desperately, her eyes going to the vehicle coming ever closer.

"Trust him," Judith insisted. "He's an extremely smart, determined man. He must have a plan."

Althea clearly wanted to believe her but was desperately afraid that she might be wrong. It was Sebastian's steady confidence that finally convinced her. "Have faith in His Highness," he said gently. "He is a great leader, and he will save us."

Another blast of rifle fire cut off further discussion. They hunkered down behind the outcropping, and Louis barked an order to his men. Judith didn't have to be able to see to know what was happening. Several of the terrorists would be slipping around the ledge, moving into position to shoot them.

But before that could happen, the vehicle moved into Louis's line of vision, and he abruptly called for the firing to stop. His problem was clear: He had to be able to produce Althea in order to carry out his plan; it would not avail him to be seen shooting her.

A man stepped from the vehicle and stood staring up toward the ledge. He raised his right arm, at the end of which fluttered a white pennant.

"Hold your fire," Louis ordered. "Let him come closer."

But instead of doing so, the man waited where he was. Louis cursed harshly. "Althea is here," he shouted. "She is safe. Come up and see for yourself."

The man began to take a step forward, only to stop when Althea screamed. "No, Gregory don't! They mean to kill you!"

"It's you or her!" Louis shouted, throwing deception to the winds. "She has only minutes to live unless you surrender, Gregory. Do you want to see her die?"

"Don't do it!" Althea pleaded. She jumped up, clearly intending to draw fire away from the man she loved.

But before she could do so, Judith lunged, pulling her back down even as bullets whizzed over their heads, only to stop an instant later as gunfire erupted from the mouth of the cave. There were anguished screams from the duke's men as they tried desperately to flee. Louis himself fell with a bullet in his shoulder. In a matter of moments, the terrorists were overrun by a troop of the Royal Hussars, led by Gregory himself.

The young king stood over the supine body of his cousin, looking down at him grimly. "So, Louis, it has come to this."

Far from repentant, the duke snarled back at him. Clasping his bleeding shoulder, he said, "It was my duty to try to overthrow you. You will destroy Gregoria."

"No," Gregory said softly, "but I will give our people the chance to grow, in safety and in peace."

He turned away and crossed the short distance to where Judith, Althea and Sebastian had emerged from behind the outcropping. For a moment he and his young fiancée simply looked at each other. Then she was in his arms, held close in his embrace, and everyone else was suddenly very busy looking elsewhere.

Judith, in particular, focused her attention on the man in the Royal Hussar's uniform who had distracted Louis for the vital minutes necessary to bring the king and his men through the cave.

Gavin flashed her a cheery grin as he climbed up the hill to her side. "Bit more eventful than the usual diplomatic maneuvering, but I have to admit, I got a kick out of it."

"I'm so glad," she said grimly. "You could also have gotten your fool head shot off."

Precisely the point Gregory had made when he tried to talk him out of it. There were men in the security force who could have stood in for the king, but Gavin had insisted on being the one to do it. He couldn't bring himself to trust anyone else with Judith's life.

Rather than dwell on any of that, he said lightly, "I know the range of their weapons, and I stayed just out of reach."

"It was still a hell of a risk to take." Her stomach churned at the very thought of it. Now that the crisis was over, reaction was setting in. She sat down abruptly on a nearby rock, a moment before her knees would have given way.

"Surely," she said, "this goes beyond the usual duties of an American ambassador."

Gavin sat down beside her and put an arm around her shoulders, ignoring her stiffness. "I was here in a different capacity," he explained.

"Oh, really?" She sniffed and kept her face turned away from him. "What was that?"

"The same as Gregory, as a man determined to protect the woman he loves."

"Oh . . ."

"You do understand what I'm telling you, Judith?"

"I've never been accused of being dense."

"Good," he said with satisfaction.

Her throat was very thick. The tears she had tried so hard to prevent fell unbidden. "No," she whispered, "not good at all." All the pain and anguish she felt was in her eyes as she said, "There's no future for us, Gavin. It was wrong of me to ever let you think there might be."

Chapter 17

"You did a great job," Sam Wexman said. They were sitting in his office high above the Manhattan street. He had his feet up on the huge marble desk and was puffing away on a cigar, something he indulged in only when he was feeling *very* good.

Judith was less content. She had been listening to Sam praise her to the skies for five minutes now, all the while thinking only of how soon she could get away. Anything to do with Gregoria and the events of the last few weeks hurt her terribly.

But of course, Sam had no way of knowing that. All he was aware of was that their network had been the first to break the xanium story, going on the air with it the moment the agreements were signed. Better yet, they had had an exclusive on the inside story of the attempted coup d'etat, including private interviews with both the king and his new queen.

In the process, they had beaten out every other representative of the worldwide media, including one Jim West, who had been laid up in a Gregorian hospital nursing a concussion after being clobbered over the head by the terrorists. Mr. West had tried to salvage the situation by claiming to have inside information about gold smuggling in Gregoria, but no one believed him. Hadn't the king himself announced that there was no such smuggling, only a network of enterprising businessmen who deserved their government's support?

Next to all that, the coverage of the wedding had seemed the icing on the cake, but that too had gone extremely well. They'd had a record-setting audience for the actual wedding ceremony, by which time details of the attempts on Gregory's and Althea's lives had been broadcast. It seemed that everyone really did love a happy ending.

Which did not explain why Judith was looking so down in the dumps these days.

"Yes, sir," he said, "you can pretty well write your own ticket from now on. Anything you want, just tell me." He waited, well aware that he had voluntarily put himself way out on a limb, but confident that he really would deliver on anything she asked for.

"Oh," Judith said, "thanks. If I think of anything, I'll let you know."

"If you think of anything... Hey, that doesn't sound right. What about money, power, glory, the anchor chair? It's all yours for the asking."

"Hmmm, that's nice." She knew she wasn't reacting correctly, but couldn't seem to do anything about it. A week ago she would have leaped head first at Sam's offer, using the opportunity to sew up the anchor job. Now all she could think of was going home and finding some way to distract herself from another empty evening.

"I think I'll get rid of some paperwork," she said. "Make some inroads on the piles on my desk. Unless," she added hopefully, "you've got something else for me to do?" If only he could come up with a really difficult assignment, preferably on the other side of the earth. *That* she would jump at.

"No," Sam said slowly, eyeing her through the cloud of cigar smoke. "Go ahead, do your paperwork. Maybe we can get a bite to eat later."

"Sure," she said, though she had no appetite. In the week since the abrupt end of Louis's attempt to overthrow his royal cousin, she had tried desperately to concentrate on her work and block out all else. Above all, she had been frantic to avoid any further contact with Gavin after their brief meeting on the hillside.

He was hurt and, she suspected, angry. Several times he had tried to see her, only to have her adroitly avoid him. At the wedding, their eyes had met once, briefly, before she tore hers away.

Since returning to New York two days before, she had heard nothing from him. That, she told herself, was what she wanted. She would fall back into the established pattern of her life. Her enthusiasm for her career would revive, and she would bury herself in her work as she had always done. Given enough time, the pain would at least become bearable. In a century or two.

Back in her office she sat slumped in her chair, staring sightlessly at the mounds of letters, memos, reports, and so on that had accumulated during her absence. Eventually she had to wade through them, but it was next to impossible to muster the energy.

At length, she forced herself to start going through the nearest pile, only to stop when she realized it consisted of congratulations from viewers for the excellent job she'd done in Gregoria. Much as she appreciated people taking the time to write, she couldn't bring herself to read them.

She had a bit more luck with the interoffice memos about other stories that were in the works, but not even they could hold her attention. Over and over her eyes strayed to the front page of that morning's newspaper, which carried a photograph of Gavin with the story announcing his new appointment as a special presidential advisor on foreign affairs, to be based in Washington.

Painful though it had been, she had read the story with a sense of relief that he was in no way being penalized for not completely succeeding in his mission in Gregoria. Rather than grant exclusive use of the xanium to the United States, Gregory had decided to make it available to the USSR and Western Europe as well.

But before a single ounce of the precious isotope would be released, a combined panel of scientists, diplomats, and politicians from all the countries involved had to work out a plan for a shared nuclear defense.

There would be no competitive systems, no risk that one nation would acquire protection from nuclear weapons at the cost of others. On the contrary, they would have to learn a new spirit of cooperation as part of putting an end forever to the threat of nuclear destruction.

Undoubtedly, it would take longer that way, but the results in the end would be far more lasting. Surprising though Gregory's decision had been, no one protested. There was a dawning sense of a corner turned, of hope suddenly found, and of a dream of peace that could truly become a reality.

So much for the fate of the world. She had her own to worry about.

A heavy sigh escaped her. She was deep-down tired in a way that had nothing to do with physical weariness. It was fatigue of the heart and of the spirit. Worse yet, she was slowly coming to the conclusion that she had acted in a cowardly manner, hurting the man she loved rather than risking exposing her own hurt to him.

Maybe it wasn't too late. She could at least call him, explain why she had done what she had, and ask him to understand. Undoubtedly, he would pity her, but she could live with that if she had to.

She was staring at the telephone, trying to decide what to do, when a sudden, tingling sense of awareness pierced her consciousness.

Gavin was standing in the doorway to her office. He was casually dressed in slacks and a sport coat. His hair was, as always, rumpled. He looked tired, and determined.

"Mind if I come in?" he asked.

Hardly believing what she was seeing, she held out a shaky hand to the visitor's chair across from her desk. "N-no... of course not."

"I wasn't sure," he said as he sat down. "You're very good with the cold shoulder."

"Please..." It seemed so childish, but she simply couldn't stand his being mean to her, no matter how justified it might be.

Gavin's taut features abruptly softened. He looked at her with surprise and something else that could have been hope. "Judith... I know you don't have any obligation to me, but please... tell me what went wrong with us." More harshly, he added, "It's driving me crazy."

She took a deep breath and gathered together what she could of her shattered courage. Slowly, she said, "I know I shouldn't have left Gregoria without talking with you. But it's so hard...."

"Why?" he asked gently. "We haven't had any problems communicating."

The memory of exactly how well they had done so made her blush. That, in turn, brought a gleam to

Gavin's eyes, and with the mood between them some-what lightened, they even managed to laugh.

"No," Judith said with a shaky smile, "we haven't. In fact, I've...uh...never communicated quite so thoroughly before."

"Neither have I. No," he went on when he saw her surprise, "not even with Carrie. What we shared was wonderful, but I'm a different person now, older and more mature. Because of that, I'm more capable of feeling and," he added, "of understanding."

He had given her the opening; now all she had to do was take it. Slowly, she said, "You love Jessie and Davey very much, don't you?"

Puzzled, he nodded. "Yes, but what does that have to do with—"

"Please, let me finish. You're a wonderful father, and I imagine that if you ever did marry again, you'd want to have more children."

"I suppose..." he said, still not understanding her. She watched as that changed, and the light of com-prehension dawned in him. "That's what upset you..." he murmured, staring at her. "You're afraid you can't have children."

Sadly, she shook her head. "No, it's worse than that. I know I can't have any."

"But why?" The words were blurted out in his shock. He was leaning forward in the chair, his hands clasped, gazing at her intently.

This was the moment she had dreaded, the one she had shied away from all her adult life. Since she'd been in the hospital, she had never spoken of the bitter grief that had shaped her. Now, as she struggled to do so at last, the words came painfully.

"When I was twenty years old," she said, "I was dating a young man I met at college. We'd been going out a few weeks when he took me to a party. He got drunk, and I didn't have the sense to refuse to get back in the car with him. He was driving me back to the dorm when he ran a red light and slammed into a truck."

Gavin's intent silence forced her to continue. "He wasn't hurt," she said with a dry laugh, "and neither was the truck driver, fortunately. But I was critically injured, and when I finally came to in the hospital, it was to the news that because of the internal damage that had been done and the surgery the doctors had to perform to save my life, I would never be able to have any children."

"I'm sorry," he murmured.

"Don't be. I have a great deal to be happy about: a wonderful career, a life many people would envy. Say, did you know I've got a good shot at the anchor job?"

"That's terrific, but—"

"No buts. Look, Gavin, what we had was great, but it's over. I realize that, so—"

"Why?" he demanded, rising and coming around the desk to where she was sitting.

"Wh-why what?" He looked very big as he loomed over her, and unless she very much missed her guess, he was angry again.

"Why is it over? Just because you can't have kids?"

"*Just* because? I'd say that's a pretty good reason."

"I'd say it's a load of bull." He reached down and, without ceremony, hauled her up to face him. "I can't believe that you could be so incredibly stupid, so shallow, so insensitive, as to risk wrecking both our lives over something so inconsequential."

Never in her wildest dreams could she have imagined anyone using such a word to describe the burden she had borne for so many years. Her temper flared, washing out the aching grief that had plagued her ever since she'd left Gregoria. "Talk about insensitive," she shot back. "If you had any feelings at all, you'd know how devastating it was for me. I felt as though I wasn't a real woman, as though I had nothing to offer a man."

"And you still feel that way," he said grimly. "That's why you're still running."

"No," she said more calmly. "I don't. I have a great deal going for me, but I'm a realist. If I'd had the luck to fall in love with a man who didn't care about children, it would be different."

"In love?"

"That's obvious."

"Not really—you have a funny way of showing it." His mouth grew suddenly tender, turning up at the corners, though his eyes remained watchful. "Or maybe you don't. You really thought you were protecting me, didn't you? Almost like Althea protected Gregory."

"I suppose so...." She wished he would let go of her, and she hated the thought that he might. Treacherously, she yearned for just another moment close to him, safe in his arms, cherished as only he had ever made her feel.

"No suppose about it." Gently, he lifted her chin, compelling her to look at him. "Judith, listen to me. I have two children I love dearly, and who incidentally are crazy about you. But if I didn't have any, I would still love you and want you to be my wife. The fact that you can't give birth doesn't make you any less a woman."

"I know people say that, but—"

"I'm not 'people,'" he said. "I'm the man who loves you, and I damned well am not leaving this office until you realize what that means. I love *you*, Judith, not some hypothetical children we might or might not have ever had together."

Tremulous hope was rising in her. She wanted so desperately to believe him, yet she was terribly afraid to do so. "Gavin, what if you're wrong? What if we did get married and afterward you decided that you really wanted more children?"

"First, it isn't something I'd decide on my own. We'd do it together. And if it was what we both wanted, what would be wrong with adoption? My God, when I think of some of the places I've been and the children I've seen in desperate need of good homes. What's wrong with giving a child a chance it wouldn't have otherwise?" He looked at her searchingly. "Or do you have the idea that you couldn't love an adopted child as well as you would one you gave birth to?"

"No, of course not," she assured him. It hadn't even occurred to her that there could be a difference in the quality of such love. A child was, after all, a child, however it had come to be. "I would love any child that was mine," she said sincerely.

"Good, because Jessie and Davey need your love as much as I do. They've been without a mother a long time." Very tenderly, he wiped away the tears that had begun to trickle down her cheeks. Tears of emerging happiness.

"Marry me, Judith, and I promise you all the on-the-job training you could possibly want. Then, a few years from now, if we both agree, we'll bring another child into our lives. A child that, I promise you, will be in every way our own."

She believed him. There was no doubting the truth of what he said, or his conviction. He loved her, and the dark shadow that had lain over her life for so long could not survive the light of that love. It had disappeared as surely as the long-aching pain deep inside her soul had also vanished.

She lifted her head, eager for his kiss, and would have received it if there hadn't been a discreet cough from the doorway.

"I'm buying a lock for that thing," she muttered as they both turned to find Sam smiling at them benignly.

"Sorry," he said with no hint of true repentance, "but I was just passing by and couldn't help but overhear. I suppose you'll be wanting some time off, Judith?''

"Yes, I will," she said firmly, "starting right now."

"Good, but before you go, let's get straight on that anchor job. You still want it?''

She did—it would be the pinnacle of her career—but the anchor was traditionally in New York, and Gavin was in Washington. Thoughts of a commuting marriage flashed through her mind, making her frown.

"Before you say anything," Sam cautioned, "I think I ought to tell you we're planning a major programming change. The media's too concentrated in New York. It gives us a limited perspective. So we're moving the nightly news to Washington. Do I take it you wouldn't have an objection to relocating?''

Through her smile she said, "You take it right, Sam. Washington is a great place for an anchor.''

"Hmmm," he agreed with a grin for them both, "and for a few other things, it looks like."

"Thanks, Sam," Gavin told him, holding out a hand. "You'll be at the wedding, I hope."

"Be at it? Heck, I'm going to cover it. It's too good a story to pass up. Isn't it wonderful," he went on as he left them, his voice fading down the corridor, "young love, romance in bloom, to have and to hold? Sweet heaven, it's enough to make anyone believe in happy endings.''

The two left behind him, close in each other's arms, agreed.